Tyler said gruffly.

She almost laughed out loud. "You? I don't think so."

His light blue eyes were full of indignation when he looked at her. "As your instructor I was responsible for seeing that you didn't get hurt. You can trust me. I'm not going to make any moves on you, if that's what you're worried about."

For heaven's sake, the man was serious. Tyler Jackson was too domineering, too patronizing, too darn arrogant, and he would drive her crazy. But what alternative did she have? She ignored the little voice that warned her she would live to regret her decision.

She also ignored the sudden thumping of her heart at the thought of being alone with the rugged cop in her tiny apartment. It was only for a few days. She could survive for a few days.

"All right," she said, looking him straight in the eye. "I accept your offer...."

Dear Reader,

The wonder of a Silhouette Romance is that it can touch *every* woman's heart. Check out this month's offerings—and prepare to be swept away!

A woman wild about kids winds up tutoring a single dad in the art of parenthood in *Babies, Rattles and Cribs... Oh, My!* It's this month's BUNDLES OF JOY title from Leanna Wilson. When a Cinderella-esque waitress—complete with wicked stepfamily!—finds herself in danger, she hires a bodyguard whose idea of protection means making her his *Glass Slipper Bride,* another unforgettable tale from Arlene James. Pair one highly independent woman and one overly protective lawman and what do you have? The prelude to *The Marriage Beat,* Doreen Roberts's sparkling new Romance with a HE'S MY HERO cop.

WRANGLERS & LACE is a theme-based promotion highlighting classic Western stories. July's offering, Cathleen Galitz's *Wyoming Born & Bred,* features an ex-rodeo champion bent on reclaiming his family's homestead who instead discovers that home is with the stubborn new owner...and her three charming children! A long-lost twin, a runaway bride...and *A Gift for the Groom*—don't miss this conclusion to Sally Carleen's delightful duo ON THE WAY TO A WEDDING.... And a man-shy single mom takes a chance and follows *The Way to a Cowboy's Heart* in this emotional heart-tugger from rising star Teresa Southwick.

Enjoy this month's selections, and make sure to drop me a line about *why* you keep coming back to Romance. We want to fulfill *your* dreams!

Happy reading,

Mary-Theresa Hussey

Mary-Theresa Hussey
Senior Editor, Silhouette Romance
300 East 42nd Street, 6th Floor
New York, NY 10017

Please address questions and book requests to:
Silhouette Reader Service
U.S.: 3010 Walden Ave., P.O. Box 1325, Buffalo, NY 14269
Canadian: P.O. Box 609, Fort Erie, Ont. L2A 5X3

THE MARRIAGE BEAT

Doreen Roberts

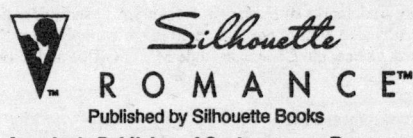

Published by Silhouette Books
America's Publisher of Contemporary Romance

If you purchased this book without a cover you should be aware that this book is stolen property. It was reported as "unsold and destroyed" to the publisher, and neither the author nor the publisher has received any payment for this "stripped book."

To Bill, for putting up with me.

I love you.

 SILHOUETTE BOOKS

ISBN 0-373-19380-7

THE MARRIAGE BEAT

Copyright © 1999 by Doreen Roberts

All rights reserved. Except for use in any review, the reproduction or utilization of this work in whole or in part in any form by any electronic, mechanical or other means, now known or hereafter invented, including xerography, photocopying and recording, or in any information storage or retrieval system, is forbidden without the written permission of the editorial office, Silhouette Books, 300 East 42nd Street, New York, NY 10017 U.S.A.

All characters in this book have no existence outside the imagination of the author and have no relation whatsoever to anyone bearing the same name or names. They are not even distantly inspired by any individual known or unknown to the author, and all incidents are pure invention.

This edition published by arrangement with Harlequin Books S.A.

® and TM are trademarks of Harlequin Books S.A., used under license. Trademarks indicated with ® are registered in the United States Patent and Trademark Office, the Canadian Trade Marks Office and in other countries.

Visit us at www.romance.net

Printed in U.S.A.

Books by Doreen Roberts

Silhouette Romance

Home for the Holidays #765
A Mom for Christmas #1195
In Love with the Boss #1271
The Marriage Beat #1380

Silhouette Intimate Moments

Gambler's Gold #215
Willing Accomplice #239
Forbidden Jade #266
Threat of Exposure #295
Desert Heat #319
In the Line of Duty #379
Broken Wings #422
Road to Freedom #442
In a Stranger's Eyes #475
Only a Dream Away #513
Where There's Smoke #567
So Little Time #653
A Cowboy's Heart #705
Every Waking Moment #783
The Mercenary and the Marriage Vow #861
*Home Is Where the Cowboy Is #909
*A Forever Kind of Cowboy #927

*Rodeo Men

DOREEN ROBERTS

lives with her husband, who is also her manager and her biggest fan, in the beautiful city of Portland, Oregon. She believes that everyone should have a little adventure now and again to add interest to their lives. She believes in taking risks and has been known to embark on an adventure or two of her own. She is happiest, however, when she is creating stories about the biggest adventure of all—falling in love and learning to live happily ever after.

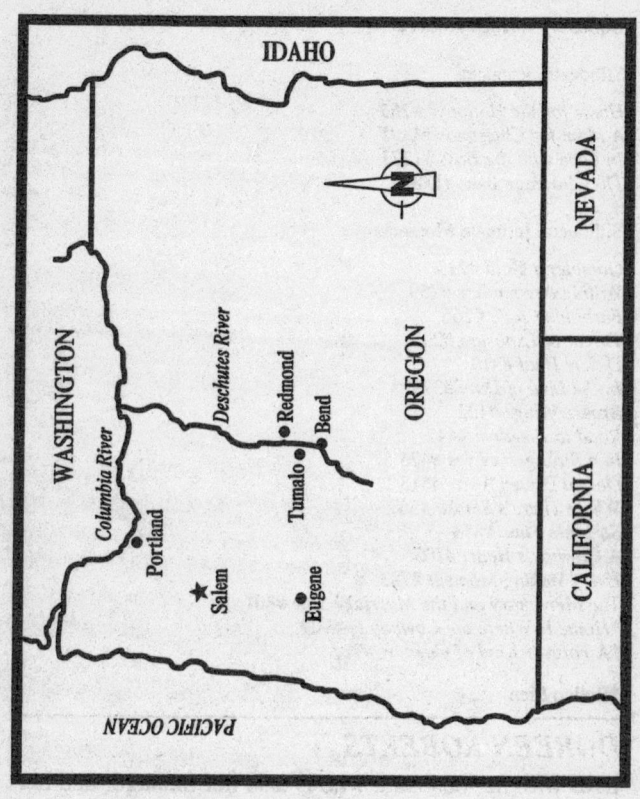

Chapter One

Trouble, Tyler Jackson reflected, usually came in threes. It didn't help matters to be lying flat on his back on the cold hard floor of Central Precinct when that profound thought occurred to him.

The sudden blow to his midriff, which had put him in that embarrassing position, was trouble number one. The young woman scrambling off his stomach was definitely trouble number two. He hated to imagine what might be trouble number three.

"I'm sorry," the woman said breathlessly. "I didn't see you until it was too late. Are you all right?"

Of course he wasn't all right. She'd barreled around the corner at sixty miles an hour and plowed straight into his stomach. The collision had knocked them both off balance and the polished floor had done the rest. He was still trying to get his wind back.

"I was in a hurry. I need help."

Tyler looked up at his assailant. She wore a sea-green silky shirt with a black skirt that rose several inches above her knees. Her shirt matched her eyes. Gorgeous eyes. He forced his attention off that fact and concentrated instead on the distress he saw in them.

Using his hands, he lithely propelled himself back on his feet. The young woman looked impressed and he was momentarily distracted. Pulling himself together he asked abruptly, "What's the trouble then? Are you hurt?"

She shook her head. "No, I'm all right. It's my purse. A man snatched it right off my shoulder." She grabbed his arm and tugged at it. "Come on, he'll get away with it if you don't hurry."

"Now just a minute...take it easy." Tyler pulled his arm free. "I need to know exactly what happened."

"I've just told you what happened." She waved an impatient hand at the door. "A man stole my purse. I need someone to go after him and get it back. Right now."

He pulled his notebook from his pocket. "Now just calm down and tell me where this happened."

"It was on the South Park Blocks. But he's not there now. He went down an alleyway on Park. If you'd just go after him he might still be there."

Tyler's first instinct was to find someone else to take the case. Anyone else. This woman was trouble. It wasn't just her silky blond hair, or her full, warm lips and mouth-watering figure, though that was a deadly enough combination. It was her tone of voice.

If there was one thing Tyler had learned to avoid, it was a pushy female, and this one had all the earmarks of a bulldozer temperament.

Deliberately he poised his pencil over the pad. "What did he look like?"

"About five-eight or nine, skinny, dressed in jeans

and a dark jacket." She paused, frowning in concentration, then went on, "He has long, dark, straggly hair and needs a shave and a good wash by the looks of him. I'll know him when I see him, I can promise you. Please, hurry." A note of desperation crept into her voice. "I can't lose my purse.... I just can't. My whole life is in there."

Her sudden look of vulnerability struck home. Instincts or not, this woman was in trouble and it was his duty to help. He happened to be on his way out anyway, he argued with his conscience as he snatched a pair of keys from the board on the wall and headed for the door.

Outside in the hot summer afternoon, he was halfway down the steps before she caught up with him. "Wait a minute. I'm coming with you," she announced, with a note in her voice that dared him to refuse.

He was tempted to do just that. One look at her stricken face, however, and he relented. "All right. You can show me where he went." He led her around the back of the building, did a fast check of the squad car, then opened the door on the passenger side. "Get in."

For a moment she looked a little apprehensive, but then she slid into the seat and sat back, her shoulders hunched.

He climbed in beside her with a sense of impending disaster, though he wasn't sure what prompted the feeling. He reached for his radio and called in his report, then started the engine. "I'm Officer Jackson," he said, as he backed the car out of its space. "I didn't get your name."

"It's Megan Summers."

"All right, Megan, where did you say this incident happened?"

"On the South Park Blocks, just off Clay." Her jaw was tense, he noticed, and her hands were thrust between her knees below the hem of her short black skirt. "I chased after him all the way down to Park, but then he went down an alley and I lost sight of him."

Tyler frowned. "You went after him? That was a mistake. You should never attempt to apprehend a criminal. You must always assume that the suspect is armed and ready to use deadly force."

"I wasn't going to apprehend him. I just wanted to see where he went."

"That's just as dangerous. If he realizes you're following him, he could easily take a shot at you to slow you down. That's a sure way of getting yourself killed."

She gave him a mutinous scowl. "I'm not a child. I can take care of myself."

He smiled. "Lady, no woman is capable of taking care of herself on the streets. Or few men for that matter."

Her expression told him she was unconvinced. "This is Portland, Oregon. You make it sound like one of those big-city slums."

"When you're facing a hunted man with a gun, it could be an amusement park for all the difference it makes." He braked at the light and sent her a stern look. "A bullet can kill you just as dead."

She lifted her chin. "Well, I think you're overreacting. I didn't see any gun. I knew what I was doing."

That he doubted very much. All his earlier instincts had been on the button. This woman could be trouble.

There was nothing more dangerous than a vulnerable woman who believed she was invincible. Especially one who refused to be convinced otherwise.

Obviously Ms. Summers resented being told what was good for her. He'd met women like her before. In fact he'd married one. The fact that the marriage had ended in disaster just went to prove he knew what he was talking about.

Giving up the argument for the time being, he pulled out into the middle lane. "We'll cruise the streets for a while, but I doubt if we'll spot him now."

"We must find him. I absolutely refuse to let him have my purse."

"Is there anything else you can tell me about him?"

"Nothing other than what I've already told you."

"Then tell me again." He listened to her description, his gaze raking the street on both sides as he drove up Main.

"I lost him when he turned down there," she said, waving her hand at the corner, where a large truck was just backing out of the loading zone.

Tyler waited for the truck to pull out, then followed it around the corner. The main rush of the lunch hour was over, but there were still enough people hurrying down the sidewalks to make it difficult to pick out an alleged purse snatcher.

"I doubt if we'll spot him now," he said, after they'd driven several blocks. "He's had too much time to go underground."

She looked annoyed. "There must be something you can do. Can't you call in some help or something?"

He hadn't really expected to spot the suspect. Too much time had elapsed and there had been too many places to hide. He'd done his best with what little he'd had to go on, and he resented the implication that he was shirking his duty.

"I've done all I can for the time being," he said evenly. "I've investigated the scene. Now we'll go back to the station and fill out a report. I'll give you some mug shots to look at and see if you can pick him out."

There was no mistaking the antagonism in her voice when she answered him. "Meanwhile he's out there spending my money. Besides, I'm supposed to be back at work. I'm real late as it is."

"I'm sure they'll understand when you explain the situation." The light ahead of him turned green and he stepped on the accelerator. Out of the corner of his eye he saw her hands curl into small fists. She wore no ring on her third finger, he noticed.

"Reports are not going to get my purse back. I'd rather be out on the streets looking for the man."

"Risking your life. Not to mention the lives of other people who might be in the line of fire. I suggest you leave the police work to the people who are qualified to do it."

She started to say something, bit back the words, then said carefully, "I'm afraid I don't have time to fill out your reports. You can drop me off right here, thank you."

He could just imagine the effort it had taken her to control her temper. He almost felt sorry for her. "Well, Ms. Summers, I'm afraid I'll have to insist. A crime has been committed and it's my duty to do everything I can to apprehend the suspect. If you have any hopes at all of recovering your property, I suggest you cooperate with me. I promise you I'll be just as quick as I can."

She slumped back against the seat so hard she jarred his shoulders. She kept quiet, however, and he pursed his lips in satisfaction. First round to him.

Megan was still fuming by the time they reached the station. Officer Jackson, she decided, had to be the most arrogant, patronizing, overbearing cop on the force. Trust her luck to be stuck with someone like him. She followed him into a noisy room filled with desks and people, resenting every step. It was really too bad that a man with his looks should be so downright domineering.

He wasn't all that tall, about five-ten she figured, but he had the kind of athletic build that took lots of strenuous work to maintain. She couldn't help noticing that the pants of his uniform fitted snugly across his hips, and his waistline was firm above his belt.

She let her gaze travel up his back to his straight dark hair. He'd worn sunglasses in the car, but she knew his eyes were a kind of silvery-blue. She could still remember the way he'd stared up at her when he was sprawled on the floor.

She felt bad about that now. She'd been in such a hurry to find a cop to help her she'd raced around the corner without stopping to think that someone might be coming the other way. She'd just about slammed all the breath out of her lungs when she'd smacked into his hard chest.

His feet had slipped on the polished floor and helped by her weight, they had both gone crashing down. She'd landed on top of him, and heard his grunt as her elbow dug into his stomach. The memory of his solid body underneath her was still vivid in her mind. In fact, thinking about it now sent a tingle down her back.

Officer Jackson led her to a desk in the corner of the

room. "Take a seat, Ms. Summers." He pointed to one of the office chairs facing the desk.

"Thank you." She sat on the edge of the chair, her gaze drawn to the framed certificates on the wall behind the desk. There were photos, as well...and she spotted a picture of Officer Jackson shaking hands with another police officer.

"Now, let's see." He sat down at the desk and opened a drawer. "We'll start with your name, address and phone number." He pulled his notebook from his pocket and dropped it on the desk.

She gave him her address, realizing as she did so that all her identification had vanished along with her purse. Driver's license, social security card, credit cards... "I have to put a stop on my credit cards," she said, interrupting his next question.

"All in good time. Where do you work?"

"I'm a travel agent at the Starways Travel Agency. Or I was as of this morning."

He ignored her wry comment and scribbled something down on his notepad. "What time did this incident occur?"

"About an hour ago." She glanced up at the large clock on the wall above his head. "He's had plenty of time to max out all my cards by now."

"You won't be held responsible for the charges," Tyler Jackson murmured.

"I'm responsible for the first fifty on each one. That's going to add up."

Relenting, he waited impatiently while she made the necessary calls.

As she finished the last one, a disturbing thought

occurred to her and she looked at him in dismay. "How am I going to get in my apartment without my keys?"

"I'm sure the manager will have a spare. Can you repeat the description you gave me one more time?"

She did so, rapidly and with rising resentment. He was taking this all very calmly, she thought, considering she'd been attacked in broad daylight on a downtown street. It was all right for Officer Jackson, he hadn't just had his most valuable personal possessions stolen, with apparently little hope of getting them back.

The questions seemed endless, and for the most part pointless. With one eye on the clock, Megan answered them, feeling more and more frustrated with each passing minute. She'd be real lucky to have a job to go back to, she thought sourly, if this idiot didn't quit with his ridiculous questions.

It was hard to concentrate in the noisy room, where several people seemed to be talking at once. Phones rang constantly, and the big burly cop standing by the door kept throwing glances her way, as if he were trying to listen in on the conversation.

"How much cash were you carrying?" Tyler Jackson asked, his pen poised above the notepad.

Her patience finally expended, Megan threw up her hands. "What difference does it make? It's all gone by now, isn't it? Is all this going to get my purse back? Or what's left of it?"

"Probably not."

"Then why are we wasting time? We could have found the man by now if we'd stayed out there looking for him, instead of filling out all this useless information."

The silver-blue eyes regarded her with faint hostility. "This may seem useless to you, Ms. Summers, but every tiny detail is important. Even if we had found the man, there's no guarantee I could have arrested him. We have to follow procedure in these cases."

The enormity of her loss was just beginning to make itself known. Her bank accounts were probably empty by now, which meant bounced checks, embarrassing explanations, more endless forms and phone calls. She glared at Tyler Jackson as if it were all his fault. "I just don't think you fully understand what it means to lose all your identification, not to mention a sizeable chunk of your finances."

"I understand that you're upset, but unfortunately once in a while stuff happens. Don't you have any family who can help you out for the time being?"

"My mother lives on the other side of town and has her own problems. I'm not going to burden her with mine."

"Well, you're lucky. Lots of people don't have that much."

Including him, she guessed, sensing the bitterness behind that comment. He looked down at his notepad and gave his head a slight shake, as if disturbed by his own words. "I'll get the mug shots," he said, and pushed his chair back.

Megan sent another harried glance at the clock. "What are my chances of finding him in there?"

He shrugged. "Maybe one in fifty."

"That's what I figured." She stood up, feeling empty-handed without her purse to hang onto. "I'm sorry I wasted your time."

His mouth tightened. "I'm sorry, too. I'd be a little more careful in future, if I were you. If you hadn't been walking around the city streets with your purse hanging conveniently over your shoulder, the snatcher might not have had such an easy time of grabbing it."

Annoyed with his condescending tone she said hotly, "Maybe if there were more cops on the streets these things wouldn't happen."

Officer Jackson leaned forward, with a menacing expression that made Megan glad she wasn't on the wrong side of the law. "This might be a safe city by most standards, but it's got its share of deadbeats waiting for a handout. They're just looking for someone like you to come along and make it easy for them."

"Well, I think there's something wrong with a city when you can't walk around without fear of being attacked by some vicious thug."

"There's a lot wrong with the world today, Ms. Summers. Which is hardly the fault of law officers. We do our best. I would suggest, however, since you seem intent on putting your life on the line, that you get your locks changed. Just in case. You might also want to take self-defense lessons. The police force offers a course every eight weeks. They could give you the edge you just might need some day."

She opened her mouth to give him a sharp answer, but then closed it again. That might not be such a bad idea. She thought about it for a moment or two. "All right, where do I sign up?"

He seemed taken aback by her question. He looked at her blankly for a moment, then glanced up at a calendar hanging on the wall next to him. "I guess you'll have to wait until the fall. The class is full right now."

"Jackson? A word with you, please?"

The command had come from the beefy cop by the door. Tyler looked over at him, and gave him a brief nod. "I'll be right back," he said to Megan. "There are a couple of things I need you to sign before you leave."

Exasperated by yet another delay, Megan watched the two men disappear out of the door. She was beginning to feel that she would never get out of that room. The picture on the wall caught her eye again and she edged around the desk to get a closer look at it.

It was a photo of Tyler Jackson receiving a citation for bravery in the line of duty. It had been taken several years ago, judging from the image of a much younger officer smiling at his superior. She had actually begun to doubt that the man could smile. He looked quite different in the picture...more carefree, and undeniably attractive without that permanent scowl on his face.

According to the certificates on the wall, Tyler had put his life on the line more than once. In spite of her irritation with him, Megan couldn't help admiring the tight-lipped cop. She'd always had a weakness for strong, dependable men, though she hadn't met too many of them as yet.

There was no doubt that Tyler Jackson was a forceful, courageous man, and she just wished she knew what had changed him from that agreeable young man in the picture to the morose, cynical cop he was today.

In fact, she thought, as she took her seat at the desk once more, if he hadn't had that annoying habit of ordering her around as if she were a teenager instead of a mature woman approaching thirty, she might be tempted to find out.

Captain Richard Stewart had always taken a personal interest in his men. It was the captain's firm opinion that a good cop needed a happy, stable home life in order to do his job. It was also his considered opinion that Tyler Jackson's home life fell far short of the ideal.

As far as Richard Stewart was aware, Tyler lived alone in a tiny studio apartment, ate mostly junk food and looked as if he could use more sleep. He rarely smiled, and the captain had never heard him joke with the rest of the guys. In other words, Tyler Jackson's life was the pits, and Captain Stewart was very much afraid that one day that pitiful state of affairs might just cause a loss of concentration and cost Tyler his life.

What Officer Jackson needed, Captain Stewart decided, was a good woman. Someone who would be strong enough to stand up to the man and make him take better care of himself. The captain had no idea if Megan Summers was that woman, but she certainly seemed to be a nice lady and undoubtedly strong-willed. After watching the two of them together, there was absolutely no doubt in the captain's mind about the spark that seemed to sizzle between the two of them.

Therefore, being the responsible captain that he was, Richard Stewart decided to take a hand in fate, so to speak, and give these two nice people a gentle nudge in the right direction. Which was why he'd called Tyler Jackson into his office.

Tyler, who was still trying to get his cool back after dealing with the argumentative Megan Summers, eyed his superior officer warily as he sat down in front of the desk. It wasn't often that he was called into the captain's office. He was trying to think of how he might have messed up.

"Jackson," Richard Stewart said, folding his hands across his protruding stomach, "I understand that young lady out there wishes to take lessons in self-defense."

Tyler nodded, wondering where this surprising statement was leading. "I told her the classes were full."

"So I heard." The captain leaned back in his chair and surveyed the ceiling. "She seems like a very independent young woman."

Tyler twisted his mouth in a wry grimace before answering, "Yes, sir. Very."

"In which case, I think she might well benefit from the lessons. Independent women have a habit of running into trouble."

"Don't I know it," Tyler muttered. "I suggested she take the classes in the fall."

"Ah." Captain Stewart appeared to think that over. "In this case, Jackson, I think it might be wise to make special arrangements for that young lady."

Tyler frowned, watching his captain with growing suspicion. "What kind of special arrangements?"

The captain lowered his chin and leaned forward. Fixing his piercing gaze on Tyler's face, he said clearly, "I think she should have the lessons now."

Tyler stared at him in bewilderment. "But the classes are full. Plus they've already started. It would throw the instructor off if Ms. Summers came in at this late date."

"Exactly, which is why I think she should have private lessons."

"Private lessons? But—"

"And you should give them to her."

Tyler's feet hit the floor as he bounced off his chair. "What? Why me? Are you nuts?"

The captain's eyes narrowed and Tyler hastily added, "Sir?"

"I'm not nuts, as you so succinctly put it," Stewart said mildly. "I happen to think that young lady would be a great deal safer if she knew how to protect herself in an emergency."

"No doubt, but surely it can wait until the fall?"

"I don't think so."

Tyler had the distinct impression that something was brewing behind the captain's stern expression, but he couldn't for the life of him think what it might be. He cleared his throat. "I'm sorry, Captain. I'd like to oblige, but my quota is full. I don't have time to give self-defense lessons to anyone right now. Maybe later on...."

Captain Stewart could look almost murderous at times. This was one of those times.

"I said now, Jackson. I suggest you find time."

Tyler made one last, desperate attempt. "But—"

"And that's an order."

Tyler clamped his lips tight shut before the curse slipped out. He waited a second or two, then muttered a quiet, "Yes, sir," before turning on his heel to head for the door.

"Jackson."

Tyler waited, his hand on the doorknob.

"This week, Jackson. No later."

This time Tyler's muttered, "Yes, sir," was delivered through gritted teeth. On his way out he shut the door with a decisive thud. The old man was losing his marbles. Private lessons in self-defense? Where in the hell was he going to find the time? Who the hell wanted to spend what little spare time he had wrestling with a smart-mouthed woman who looked as if she'd break in two if he so much as touched her?

The thought of having to throw Megan Summers

down on the floor was bad enough. The idea of teaching Megan Summers to throw *him* down on the floor was intolerable.

What was really intolerable, Tyler reluctantly admitted as he strode grimly back to the office, was that for a brief instant, when Megan Summers was scrambling to climb off him earlier, he had felt a distinct response in a place that hadn't had a whole lot of action lately.

Now he knew where trouble number three was coming from. That, as far as Tyler was concerned, was the worst trouble of all. If he had to spend the next six to eight weeks wrestling with a woman who could turn him on that easily, he was heading for total disaster.

Inside the office, Megan looked up expectantly as the door swung open. Officer Jackson walked in, looking as if he would like to mow down everyone in his path. Obviously the news had not been good. She wisely decided to keep a still tongue as he sat down heavily at the desk.

He stared down at the notepad for so long she wondered uneasily if the bad news was connected to her encounter with the purse snatcher. She was about to ask him when he tore a sheet from the notepad, and looked up with a formidable expression that made her forget what she was going to ask.

"Read this over and sign here," he said curtly, flipping the page across the desk.

She scanned the lines without comprehending what she was reading. She knew he was watching her, with a strange brooding expression that stirred up all kinds of unrest inside her. Her hand shook slightly as she picked up the pen he'd pushed across to her. Quickly she scrawled her signature and thrust the paper back at him. "Now am I free to go?"

"In just a moment." He stared down at the page in his hand as if he'd never seen it before.

He was making her nervous. Something was obviously bothering him and somehow she just knew it had something to do with her. She couldn't just sit there and wait all afternoon for him to tell her what it was.

"Officer Jackson—"

"Ms. Summers—"

They'd both spoken at once, and Megan waited, holding her breath.

"Ms. Summers," Tyler Jackson said, a little more quietly, "I have been authorized to offer you private lessons in self-defense. Starting immediately."

Of all the things she'd been expecting him to say, it certainly wasn't that. She stared at him, forgetting to close her mouth.

Tyler gave her a look filled with desperation. "Of course, you are quite at liberty to refuse—"

She said the first thing that came into her head. "Who will be giving the lessons?"

She knew by his hunted expression what the answer would be long before he blurted out, "I've been appointed your instructor."

Obviously under protest. She sat back, thinking furiously. She had no idea who had instigated this turn of events or why, but her first instinct was to refuse. Much as she would like to have the security of knowing how to protect herself, the mere thought of wrestling on a mat with the imposing, antagonistic cop was enough to turn her insides to jelly.

The fact that she felt a distinct thrill at the prospect

only intensified the problem. She didn't need any more complications in her life right now.

On the other hand, living alone did have distinct disadvantages. One of them was the feeling of vulnerability, brought home even more potently by Tyler Jackson's observations on the criminal element in Portland. It was a feeling that did not sit well with Megan.

"I accept," she said, before she could change her mind and chicken out.

Officer Jackson looked as if he were about to throw up. "Do you know Captain Stewart personally, by any chance?" he asked, his voice a little hoarse.

"No. Not that I'm aware of, anyway. Why?"

He shook his head. "Forget it." He stared at the calendar, looked back at her, then back at the calendar again. "How does Thursday night sit with you?"

"Thursday night's just fine. Where?"

"The gym." He scribbled down an address on a small yellow notepad. "Can you make it by six? We'll have an hour before the volleyball team takes over."

"I'll be there." She took the note and glanced at it. "Thank you, Officer Jackson."

He passed a hand across his brow, sweeping back his hair. "Look...Megan, it will make things a lot easier if you just call me Tyler."

He'd called her Megan earlier, she remembered. Then he'd changed it to Ms. Summers. Now he was back to calling her Megan again. She liked that a whole lot better. "Thank you, Tyler. You'll let me know if you find my purse?"

He started, as if he'd forgotten why she was there in the first place. "Of course. Though I wouldn't hold out too much hope if I were you. We rarely recover snatched purses, and even if we do, they are generally empty.''

He was just a little ray of sunshine, Megan thought, as she walked out of the office and down the hallway to the main doors. Whatever happened to positive thinking? But then, being a cop in today's violent world probably didn't allow much room for positive thoughts. More than likely, Tyler Jackson was just too busy trying to stay alive.

She walked slowly back along the six blocks to her office, aware that particular thought bothered her a great deal more than it should have. Already she was beginning to have a protective attitude toward him. This was not good.

She thought about calling him and canceling the lessons. Then she reminded herself that she was a grown woman and well able to take care of herself. If she couldn't stay indifferent to a surly cop with an attitude, then she wasn't her mother's daughter.

With that thought squarely in mind, she marched back to her office and did her best to forget the steely eyes of Officer Tyler Jackson.

Chapter Two

Tyler sat for a long time at his desk after Megan Summers had left, wondering what on earth had possessed his captain to order such a dumb assignment. Maybe he was being punished for something he didn't know about. More likely Captain Stewart was trying to prove something, though heaven knew what that was.

Tyler sighed, and slipped the report he'd just filled out into the file. He hadn't joined the force to give self-defense lessons. In fact, there were some days when he wondered why he'd ever wanted to become a cop. It certainly wasn't the glamorous, exciting life he'd imagined when he'd first started as a rookie.

The job had its moments, of course...the feeling of satisfaction of a job well done when he'd seen a criminal locked away. Watching a thug get what he deserved—those were the moments that made his job worthwhile.

There was also the downside. The innocent people hurt, maimed or killed by a lawbreaker—children on drugs, wives beaten half to death, families crushed in a car hit by a drunk driver—these were the nightmares that haunted him.

In comparison, he thought, as he scanned the information Megan Summers had given him, wrestling a defenseless woman to the mat seemed like a picnic. Even so, he wished he'd never mentioned the lessons. A little learning could be dangerous.

He could just imagine Megan Summers taking on the entire criminal population of Portland if she thought she could overpower them. He'd have to make darn sure she understood that her ability would be limited. He'd have to warn her not to start something she wasn't sure she could finish.

Tyler closed the file and dropped it into the out bin. He could understand her frustration, of course. She was a helpless victim, and she wanted to hit back. He knew that feeling very well. He'd watched his own brother struggle with his inadequacies.

Tyler had fought many a battle for Mason, defending his brother against the ignorant bullies who taunted him. It was Tyler who had been suspended from school for fighting, and it was Tyler who had been grounded for two weeks for blacking both eyes of the kid next door. He'd considered it a small price to pay for the satisfaction of teaching his brother's tormentors a lesson.

Tyler shook his head as he got wearily to his feet. That was him, the almighty protector. He'd done it so much for his brother it had become a way of life for him. And it was still getting him into trouble.

He closed his mind to the vision of a delicate face and beautiful green eyes. Megan Summers's looks were deceptive. There was nothing fragile about that lady. He was worrying over nothing. Might as well accept the situation and get it over with as quickly as possible.

He tried to keep that thought firmly in mind as he watched Megan walk across the floor toward him on Thursday evening. She was wearing black tights and a bright pink leotard that hugged her body as close as a second skin. The tiny sleeves left most of her arms bare and the scooped neckline hovered just above the line of decency. The second he saw her he knew he was in deep trouble.

He lowered his gaze to the floor and massaged the back of his neck, giving himself time to reconstruct his shattered composure. He was glad he'd put on shorts and tank top. He was going to need all the help he could get to keep his cool.

He had to force himself to look up when she reached him. If it was any comfort, she looked as nervous as he felt. She'd tied her hair back with a pale pink scarf, and wore no makeup, save for a dash of color on her lips. The effect made her look much younger than the twenty-nine years she'd stated on the report.

He was just seven years older than her, but right then the gap seemed much wider. It helped. A little. "I'm glad to see you're on time," he said, his uneasiness making his voice sound harsh.

She lifted her chin. "I'm always on time."

Her cool voice made him think of a creek trickling through the forest on a hot summer afternoon. Unnerved by his poetic thoughts, he turned away from her and waved his hand at the mat. "Okay, let's get started."

He made her stand on the very edge of the mat, as

far away from him as possible, as he went through the usual routine of explaining some of the easier ways she could defend herself. She seemed uncomfortable at his demonstration of poking fingers into an assailant's eyes or throat, and looked sick when he told her that if she thrust the heel of her hand hard enough up under an attacker's nose she could drive the bone through his brain.

That one usually got to the more squeamish students, but Megan seemed to recover fast enough to ask questions. In fact, by the time he'd finished his initial briefing of what the lessons would entail, she seemed anxious and eager to get on with them.

A glance at the clock told him he still had thirty minutes. Half an hour of pure torture, if his body was any indication of what to expect.

"Before we start the first moves," he announced, hoping his dry throat wouldn't affect his voice, "we'll do a warm-up session to relax your muscles."

"My muscles are perfectly relaxed," Megan announced, doing a swift knee-bend to prove it. "I work out every morning."

Her muscles might be perfectly relaxed, Tyler thought grimly, but his were as tight as a drum. "I don't care what you do in the mornings. When you're in my class you do warm-ups. I don't need a pulled muscle on my conscience."

Her magnificent eyes sparkled with resentment. "I'm not likely to pull a muscle, but if you insist—"

"I do insist."

She looked put out, but followed him through the warm-up routine, making it all look so effortless his normally active body felt sluggish.

When he couldn't put it off any longer, he braced

himself for the hands-on procedures. "The first thing you have to remember when attempting to use a defensive move is to act with aggression. Yell, scream or swear, but make as much noise as possible. It will unnerve your opponent." He took a stance, jabbed at the air and let out a bellow that made Megan jump backward off the mat.

Pleased that he'd got his point across, he braced himself. "Now come and take a shot at me."

She blinked, took a hesitant step forward, then stopped. "I beg your pardon?"

He pounded his chest. "Here. Come and hit me here. Use as much force as you can."

She gave her head a slight shake, poised herself on her toes, then rushed at him with a yell that would have scared Geronimo. He was so taken with her effort that he almost forgot to sidestep. Pivoting on his heel, he caught her raised arm, pulled her forward, tucked his shoulder into her armpit and bent double, flipping her neatly over his shoulder.

At least, it was supposed to be neatly. The sudden shock of her lithe body slithering over his made him check for an instant, enough to make him lose the momentum. He had to grab her to prevent her from falling awkwardly.

Luckily she didn't seem to notice as she sprawled safely and somehow elegantly onto the mat. "Wow!" she said, sitting up. "That was great. It looks so easy. Can I do that?"

Tyler was still trying to get his wits back after suffering the exquisite agony of grasping her slim waist with both hands. "Only if you pay attention to what I tell you," he barked hoarsely.

She looked taken aback at his tone, and he pulled in

a deep breath. *Get it under control, Jackson,* he warned himself. This was serious stuff. He needed his concentration.

He forced himself to speak more naturally. "What I did was use your momentum to pull you off balance. I pulled you in the direction you were already going, and the rest was leverage. It's not as easy as it looks. Here."

He grabbed her arm, frowning in the effort to think of her as a cloth dummy instead of a warm, vibrant, sweet-smelling woman.

The next ten minutes were pure hell. The more moves he showed her, and the more contact he had with her firm body, the more irritable he became. He was furious with himself, furious at his weakness, and even more furious at her for having the power to do this to him. In an effort to disguise his problem, he rapped out his orders, sounding like a sergeant major with a bad hangover.

Megan was having just as much trouble paying attention. From the moment she'd seen him standing on the mat, legs braced apart in black gym shorts and a large portion of his chest bared by a blue tank top, she'd had trouble concentrating.

Every time he came near her she jumped, and whenever he put his hands on her, she just about curled up inside. To make matters worse, he kept snapping out orders at her, making her even more nervous.

In fact her nerves were strung up so tight she just knew if he didn't quit yelling at her like that she'd explode, and tell him to forget the darn lessons. She should report him for being the worst instructor she'd ever encountered. Period.

He'd shown her how to grab his arm and pull him

forward, but when it came to getting her shoulder beneath him to flip him over, she kept forgetting to bend over at the right time.

She was getting tired, and her muscles were sore. She just couldn't wait until the lesson was over so she could go home and soak in the tub.

"All right," Tyler said, mopping his brow with the back of his hand, "we'll try it one more time then call it quits for tonight."

Wondering if he'd read her mind, she gathered up the last of her energy. This time she'd do it. Just once she'd like to see him flat on his back with her foot in his neck. She faced him, muscles tensed, ready for the attack.

He scowled at her, in his role of attacker. "Remember to yell."

He started toward her and she yelled, raising her hands to reach for his outstretched arm.

"Grab and pull," he shouted. "Get under, *under*, bend, bend...no *bend!*"

She bent. This time, for the first time, his feet left the floor. For one glorious moment she felt his weight shifting over her shoulder. In her delight she started to straighten up, then gasped as her arm twisted awkwardly under his weight. She hadn't quite got the hang of it yet, she realized in alarm.

He crashed to the mat on his back, dragging her with him. She cried out as his full weight landed on her forearm. He rolled off her in an instant, but the pain brought tears to her eyes. She sank onto the mat, cradling her arm against her body.

"Damn! I told you to bend." Tyler knelt in front of her. "Let me look."

She tried to lift her arm to show him, but it hurt to move it.

"Try wiggling your fingers," he ordered, his voice softening in sympathy.

She felt like crying as she gingerly moved her fingers. It hurt like the blazes, but they worked.

Gently, he reached for her arm and ran his warm fingers up and down it. "I don't think it's broken," he said gruffly, "but I'm taking you to the hospital to get it checked out."

"I don't think that's necessary—"

"Don't argue with me. You're going and that's the end of it."

She clamped her mouth shut.

She kept it shut all the way to the hospital, even though she was aware of the worried glances he kept sending her. She'd had trouble getting into her jeans, and he'd had to help her. It had been embarrassing to say the least. Right then she couldn't think of anything she wanted to say to him.

Tyler did all the talking when they arrived at the check-in desk in Emergency. He'd pulled on a pair of black sweatpants over his shorts, and looked more like a high-school coach than a cop. Megan noticed the skeptical way the nurse looked at him when he explained who he was.

She had to sign the form with her left hand, something she hadn't done since she was in grade school. Her effort looked unreadable, but the friendly nurse assured her it was just fine.

Told to wait in the lounge, she took a seat near the window, overlooking the parking lot. It gave her something on which to concentrate her attention.

Tyler sat down opposite her, his face creased in a

worried frown. "How's it feel?" he asked her, when she looked at him.

"Not bad," she lied. "I'm sure it will be just fine."

He looked guilty. "This is bad. I've never had a student injured before."

"It was my fault. I didn't bend properly."

"No, it was mine. I should have made sure you were following my instructions."

She shook her head at him. "No, really. Your instructions were fine. It was my fault. I forgot to stay down until you were all the way over and—"

"I'm the instructor. I'm supposed to be able to prevent you from hurting yourself."

She sat back, knowing it was useless to argue. He was determined to take the blame. She felt miserable. She was tired, hungry, in pain and felt like a prize idiot. If she hadn't been so distracted by Tyler Jackson's great muscles, if she hadn't been so conscious of his steely-blue eyes, she'd have paid more attention and this wouldn't have happened.

It would have to be her right arm, she thought in disgust. This was not turning out to be her week. First she'd had her purse stolen, which so far hadn't turned up, and now she'd wrecked her arm in her very first lesson in self-defense. What else could possibly go wrong?

"Megan Summers?"

She looked up to see a young nurse standing at the door, beckoning to her.

Tyler got to his feet.

Megan got up, too. "I'll be back in a minute," she told him.

"I'm going with you. Here, give me your purse. I'll carry it for you."

"I can carry it myself. I'll be fine."

"I want to be sure of that."

She looked up at him, ready to argue. One look at his face told her she'd be wasting her breath. Still hanging on to her purse, she followed the nurse into the cubicle with Tyler hot on her heels.

The nurse made her sit on the bed and pulled the curtain around her. Tyler hovered in the small space, looking painfully uncomfortable. Megan wondered what he'd do if she had to disrobe. Getting out of a leotard with one arm would prove to be real challenging.

She tried to think of something to say that would release the tension, but all she could think of was that she wanted him to leave. She didn't think that would help much.

Fortunately she wasn't kept waiting too long before a man who looked too young to be a doctor whisked the curtain aside. "Well, what have we here?" he asked, giving Tyler a quick up and down scrutiny. "I'm Dr. Hartford. Are you the husband?"

"Friend," Tyler said briefly.

The doctor glanced at Megan. "All right for him to stay?"

"As long as I don't have to take anything off." She avoided looking at Tyler, but she heard his slight cough.

"I don't think that's going to be necessary." The doctor took hold of her arm in a firm grasp and gently raised it. "Does that hurt?"

She shook her head.

He probed all the way down her arm with strong fingers. "All right, grasp my hand as if you're going to shake it."

She slowly closed her fingers around his. The second she tried to grip his hand major pain tore through her arm all the way up to her shoulder. She let out a small yelp.

"Ah." Dr. Hartford closed his fingers around her wrist and gave it a gentle twist. "Hurt?"

"Yes!"

She'd forced the word through gritted teeth, and she saw Tyler's shoulders hunch.

Dr. Hartford pulled her arm straight out in front of her. "Press your hand back," he ordered.

She tried, but nothing happened. Except for a white-hot heat slashing up her arm, that was. "I can't," she said, looking anxiously up at him. "Is it broken?"

The doctor shook his head. "No, but you've done some pretty good damage to your arm. Torn ligaments and, I suspect, a strained muscle. That will take a few days to heal."

"Will I be able to use it?" She looked down at the useless hand in her lap. "Look, I can wiggle my fingers."

"But it hurts to do that, right?"

She gave a miserable nod. "Right."

"Then don't do that." Dr. Hartford winked at Tyler, who didn't seem to get the joke.

Megan wasn't particularly amused, either.

"It's going to hurt for a while," the doctor said, giving her an encouraging smile. "We'll give you something to help with that. We'll also wrap the arm and put it in a sling to make things a little more comfortable. Don't try to use it under any circumstances. You'll only aggravate the problem, and if you do, you could end up doing some permanent damage." He handed her a business card. Make an appointment with my office to see me in a week. You should be feeling a lot better by then."

He nodded at Tyler, who said gruffly, "Thanks, Doc."

"Thank you," Megan echoed, her mind already grappling with the major problems her injury was about to cause.

"See you next week," Dr. Hartford said cheerfully. "The nurse will be back in a minute to wrap that arm. Take care." He disappeared through the curtain, leaving Megan alone with Tyler.

For a long moment neither of them spoke, then Tyler said quietly, "I'm sorry. I really messed things up for you."

She shook her head, her mind still on her problems. "I'll manage."

"What about your work?"

She shrugged. "I'll take a couple of weeks off."

"You're going to need some help. What about your mother? Can she take care of you?"

She looked up at him. "Look, please don't worry about me. I'll be fine. It's only one arm. I've got another one."

"It's your right arm. You're right-handed, right?"

"Yes, but—"

"You haven't begun to realize how awkward that's going to be for you. You can't drive, cut up your food, tie shoelaces, dress yourself, cook your meals or shop for groceries."

She didn't like the insinuation that she was entirely helpless. "Lots of people manage with one arm. What about all those people who lose an arm, or are born without one?"

"They've had years of therapy to learn how to get by. You're facing a crash course...alone."

He had a point. She tried to visualize herself fastening her bra with one arm. Taking the top off the toothpaste. Opening a can of soda. She let out a long sigh of frustration.

"So, what about your mother?" Tyler looked at his watch. "I could give her a call for you."

"No." Megan chewed on her lip. "My mother lives clear across town. She's a real estate agent, and relies on her commission to support herself and my kid brother. I can't take her away from her work for two weeks. She could lose customers that way."

"Couldn't you stay with her?"

"She lives in a two-bedroom apartment. Besides, she doesn't have time to take care of me. She's too busy with her own job."

Tyler started to say something else, but just then the nurse arrived to wrap her arm.

"You can shower," the nurse said, when she'd fitted the injured arm into a sling and tied it around Megan's neck, "but you will have to rewrap it afterward. Make sure it's good and tight for support."

Megan nodded. "Can I go now?"

"Sure, you can." The nurse handed her a piece of paper. "Get this filled in the pharmacy on the way out, and whatever you do, don't try to use that arm."

"I won't." Megan thanked her and slid off the bed.

The nurse smiled at them both, whisked back the curtain and hurried off to take care of someone else.

"You don't have any friends who can help out?" Tyler asked, as he walked with her down the long, brightly lit hallway.

"None who don't have full-time jobs," Megan said

gloomily. "I guess I'll have to ask my mother to step in. Much as I hate to do that."

Tyler cleared his throat. "I do have one suggestion."

She glanced up at him, but he was staring straight ahead, his jaw set at a grim angle. "What's that?"

"I could take care of you."

She almost laughed out loud. "You? I don't think so. But thanks."

His light blue eyes were full of indignation when he looked at her. "I'm quite capable of taking care of you. I have some leave due to me. I never take it, so it's adding up. I could put it to good use helping out until your arm is healed." He nodded at an arrow that pointed the way to the pharmacy. "It's down here."

She followed him, finding it hard to believe he was serious. Arriving at the counter, she handed over the prescription to a young man, who told her it would be about ten minutes.

She sat down in one of the comfortable armchairs and watched Tyler lower himself into the other. "That's very nice of you to offer," she said, still not quite sure if he was joking, "but really, I'll be fine. I'm sure my mother will be happy to have me stay there."

"Where will you sleep?"

"Gary can sleep on the couch. He's used to roughing it. He'll be okay."

"No. It was my fault you were injured. As your instructor I was responsible for seeing that you didn't get hurt. I should be the one to take care of you."

She eyed him suspiciously. "I'm not going to sue, if that's what you're worried about."

His mouth tightened. "That's not what I'm worried about. I feel bad about what happened and I want to make up for it. This is one way I can do that.'' His frown deepened. "You can trust me. I'm not going to make any moves on you, if that's what you're worried about.''

"That's not what I'm worried about.'' For heaven's sake the man was serious. She stared at him, trying vainly to think of a way to let him down lightly.

"I'm not going to take no for an answer,'' Tyler said quietly. "So don't even try.''

She said the only thing she could think of. "I only have one bedroom.''

"I'll sleep at my place, of course. But I'll be around in the daytime if you need me.''

Well, that was a relief. For a moment she thought he was proposing camping out on the floor. "I really don't think—''

"Don't think. It's all settled. I'll take you home and cook you dinner.''

"That won't be necessary. I can pick up something from a fast-food place on the way home.''

"Fast food isn't good for you. I'll cook.''

"I have to get my car from the gym.''

"I'll have one of the officers drive it over. I can take him back to his car.''

Megan stared at him, torn between a possible solution to her problem and the utter stupidity of accepting his offer. There was no way the two of them could spend five minutes in each other's company without jumping at each other's throat.

Tyler Jackson was too domineering, too patronizing, too darn arrogant, too fond of handing out orders and would drive her crazy. On the other hand, her mother would also drive her crazy. At least this way, if things got too unbearable, she could simply tell Officer Jackson to leave.

She ignored the little voice that warned her she would live to regret her decision. She also ignored the sudden thumping of her heart at the thought of being alone with the rugged cop in her tiny apartment. It was only for a few days. She could survive for a few days.

"All right," she said, looking him straight in the eye. "I accept your offer."

His steely gaze faltered for a moment, then he gave a brief nod. "Fine. I have to call the station, then I'll be right back."

She watched him disappear around the corner, wondering if it was her imagination, or if he really did look as if he were preparing for battle.

Tyler kept his head down and didn't stop until he burst through the main doors of the hospital and erupted into the parking lot.

The soft evening breeze rustled the leaves of the flowering cherry trees, cooling his brow as he strode over to his car. He needed all the help he could get, he reflected, as he unlocked the door. Of all the crazy, lamebrained ideas he'd ever had, this one had to be the absolute pits. What the hell was he thinking of?

He'd more or less made the suggestion on a wild impulse that he'd instantly regretted. When Megan Summers had refused him at first, then started to argue with him, for some reason he'd felt compelled to dig in his heels. He wasn't satisfied until he'd won the point. Now he was stuck with it.

She brought out the worst in him, he thought savagely as he reached for his cell phone. She had a way of stepping on his toes and hitting all his buttons in one go. She drove him crazy and now he would have to live with that for ten days. Maybe more. Damn the captain and his self-defense lessons. It was all his fault.

Tyler scowled as he jabbed out the captain's home phone number. He hoped Stewart was in the middle of dinner. He jumped when Lacey Stewart, the captain's wife, answered.

"It's Tyler Jackson," he said, softening his voice. "Is the captain there?"

"He's in the den," Lacey said, sounding worried. "I'll get him."

A few seconds later Stewart's voice spoke in his ear. "Jackson? What's up?"

"There's been...a little accident," Tyler said, gripping the phone with tense fingers. "I'm going to need the next couple of weeks off."

"Where are you?"

"I'm at the hospital."

"Are you hurt bad? What happened?"

Tyler sighed. "I was giving Ms. Summers her self-defense lessons, as you ordered, and I screwed up. She's hurt her arm and can't use it."

"Oh, geez." Stewart paused for a moment. "How bad is it?"

"She'll be out of action ten days or so, according to the doctor." Tyler looked up at the sky through the windshield. "I offered to take care of her," he mumbled.

"You what! Say that again, Jackson?"

Tyler gritted his teeth. "You heard me. I'm going to take care of her. She doesn't have anyone else and I feel responsible."

There was a long pause on the end of the line, then the captain spoke again with an odd tightness in his voice. "I understand. Go ahead, Jackson. Do what you have to do."

"Yes, sir. Thank you. I'll need someone to pick up her car. It's at the gym. The address is in the report of the mugging."

"I'll send someone. Just make sure he gets back to his car."

"I'll do that. Thanks, Captain."

"And...good luck, Jackson. Don't do anything I wouldn't do."

"Yeah, thanks." Tyler hung up, frowning. It sounded for all the world as if the captain was trying desperately not to laugh. The thought didn't improve his temper any.

He slammed out of the car and stood for a moment trying to calm his frisky nerves. He'd made the suggestion, and he couldn't back out now. It was true what he'd told the captain. He felt responsible.

He'd messed up and it was his moral duty to set things right. Megan Summers needed help because of something he'd done, and it was only right that he do what he could to help her out. That was all there was to it. He'd have done the same if she'd been toothless and ninety years old.

Of course, he reminded himself, as he marched back to the building, had Megan Summers been toothless and ninety years old, he wouldn't be in as much trouble as he was now.

If he were real honest with himself, he'd admit that it wasn't the way Megan Summers stirred up his irritation that bothered him half as much as the way she stirred up his primitive urges. That, he thought worriedly, was where the true problem lay and that could get him into more trouble than he could handle.

Here he was, planning on spending the next week or so in the more or less exclusive company of a woman who could make him forget all the reasons why he'd sworn off any more serious relationships. He'd just have to start thinking—and acting—like a monk for the next few days, and try not to notice that the woman drove him nuts.

Something told him that it wasn't exactly going to be a piece of cake.

Chapter Three

"I still think it would be easier just to pick up a hamburger or something," Megan said, as Tyler weaved his way through the traffic on the Banfield Freeway.

"You can't eat fast food every night for two weeks. You'll end up with stomach ulcers. If I'm going to cook for you I might as well start now."

She eyed him doubtfully. "How good a cook are you?"

"Mediocre, but I get by."

The closer they got to her apartment, the more worried she was getting. The idea of Tyler Jackson cooking dinner in her tiny kitchen gave her goose bumps. "You cook for yourself?" She'd assumed that he lived alone, but it wouldn't hurt to confirm it.

"Sometimes."

"What do you do the other times?"

He sent her a wary glance. "I eat fast food."

"How come you don't have ulcers?"

"Men have stronger stomachs than women."

And thicker heads, Megan added inwardly. She was a pretty good cook herself. She just hoped that his cooking was at least edible. "Hamburgers would be quicker," she said, refusing to give up without a fight.

"No hamburgers. You need something more nutritious than that. You're sick."

"I'm not sick. I just hurt my arm."

"You've been injured. Your resistance is down."

He was wearing it down, Megan thought mutinously. She should never have agreed to this ridiculous idea. She closed her eyes briefly as Tyler jumped lanes. For a cop he was an erratic driver. Unless all cops learned to drive that way. "I'm not sure I have anything for dinner in the fridge," she muttered, giving it one last shot.

"I'll find something." His tone warned her that was the final word.

She gave up, and spent the next five minutes trying to remember what food she had in the house that wouldn't present too much of a challenge.

"I'll need directions from here," Tyler said, as he took the off-ramp.

She gave them to him, directing him to her apartment building. He pulled up in her parking space and looked around with the same expression her mother had worn when she'd first seen it.

Annoyed with his attitude, she said defensively, "It may be small, but it's cheap and I like it." She reached across her injured arm for the door handle.

"Wait!" He shook his head at her. "I'll get that. Just sit tight."

She did her best to fight back her irritation. After all, she thought, as he leaped out of his seat and strode around to her side of the car, he was worried about her. He wanted to make sure she didn't aggravate her injury. She just wished he would give her a little more credit for taking care of things herself.

The door flew open and Tyler leaned in. "All right, feet first."

For the sake of peace she did what she was told. She swung her feet down and allowed him to take her good arm as she climbed out.

"There." He looked far too smug. "Now, where's your keys?"

"In my purse." She slipped it off her shoulder and handed it to him.

He looked at it as if it were about to explode.

"You can open it," Megan said, trying to keep the edge out of her voice. "There's nothing in there to bite you."

He sent her a scathing glance and opened the purse, dug out the keys, then handed it back to her. "All right. Which way?"

She pointed to the main door. "Through there, up the stairs and take a left. Number twenty-four."

"Got it." He took her good arm and guided her toward the door.

A couple of young women passed them on the stairs. They both gave her bandaged arm a cursory glance, then a much more thorough and appreciative inspection of the man at her side.

Megan wondered what they'd think if they knew he was a cop. She was rather glad he wasn't wearing his uniform. She had to admit, he did look quite a hunk in the tank top with his muscled torso on display. She'd probably be the talk of the second floor before the week was out. She wasn't quite sure how she felt about that.

"This it?" Tyler paused in front of her door with the key poised in his hand.

"Yes." She waited while he unlocked the door, hoping she'd left the place tidy. It seemed years since she'd left it that morning.

He stood back to let her walk in, then followed her inside and shut the door. She watched him take in his surroundings and braced herself for his comment.

His gaze wandered over the plush gold recliners, the beige tweed love seat and the desert landscape that dominated the wall behind it. She'd placed her television set and stereo against the back wall, next to the entrance to the kitchen. The hallway opposite led to her bedroom and scant bathroom.

After surveying the entire room, he gave her a brief nod. "Nice. You've made it look real cozy."

Gratified by this unexpected response, she gave him a dazzling smile. "It gets a little stuffy in here," she said, feeling awkward now that she was alone with him. "It's been shut up all day and I don't have air-conditioning."

"I'll open up the windows and get some fresh air in here."

She watched him cross the room. He seemed taller, and a lot more imposing. She just wasn't used to seeing a man in her apartment, she told herself, as she watched him raise the windows.

"Well," Tyler said, sounding just a little strained, "I guess I'd better start dinner."

"I'll help. I've got hamburger in the fridge. We can have that." She laid her purse on the small coffee table and headed for the kitchen.

"No, I can do it. I want you to sit down right here and rest that arm."

She turned to look at him. His face wore a determined expression that made the fingers of her good hand curl into a fist. "My arm is resting just fine in the sling."

"As long as I'm taking care of you, you'll have to do what you're told. Now sit down."

"There's nothing wrong with my legs. At least let me come out there and watch."

"You'll distract me. I like to cook alone." He disappeared into the kitchen and she heard him open the fridge door.

She'd known all along this was a bad idea. All right, she thought, sinking onto the love seat. Let him get on with it. After all, it wasn't every day she got waited on like this. In any case, her arm was beginning to ache.

A few seconds later, Tyler emerged from the kitchen carrying a glass of water. "Here, take your pill."

She took the glass and the pill he handed her. Trying not to resent the fact that he stood and watched her, she swallowed the capsule and handed him back the glass. "Thank you."

"Sure." He went back to the kitchen, only to return a moment later with a bottle of wine in his hand. "I found some wine. You want some?"

"I can't. I just took medication."

He stared at her for a moment, then muttered, "Right."

"You go ahead, though."

"I'd rather have a beer."

"I don't have any beer."

"So I noticed."

"I wasn't expecting company."

He gave her a disparaging look. "Well, just sit and relax. Dinner will be ready soon."

She eyed him warily. "What are you going to cook?"

"I haven't decided yet. Got a cookbook?"

"Kitchen cupboard in the corner." She frowned. "It's only hamburger. You don't have to get fancy with it. Just make patties and fry it."

He scowled at her. "If you don't mind, I'm supervising this dinner." He disappeared into the kitchen again.

Megan did her best to relax, in spite of the odd sounds coming from her kitchen. She was itching to go in there and find out what he was doing, but after hearing him curse a couple of times, decided it might be better to stay where she was.

She thought about turning on the television, to keep her mind off what was going on in her kitchen. She reached for the remote, but just then the phone rang, making her jump.

"I'll get it!" Tyler rushed out of the kitchen, face flushed and waving a wooden spoon which, Megan noticed caustically, dripped what looked like tomato juice all over the carpet.

She was tempted to point that out, but Tyler had grabbed the phone and was barking into it. "Yes?"

He waited and Megan watched his face, fascinated to know how he was going to handle this.

"Yes, it is," Tyler said, sounding impatient. "Who's calling?" Another short pause and then, "I'm a friend of Megan's.... Er...we met a couple of days ago.... No, I'm a police officer.... Here, I'll let her explain. I'm in the middle of cooking dinner."

He handed the phone over with a harried look on his face. "Your mother."

Megan hid a grin as she took the phone. "Hi, Mom."

Tyler pulled a face and fled back to the kitchen.

"Why is a police officer cooking dinner in your apartment?" her mother asked, obviously intrigued.

Megan did her best to sound matter-of-fact. "I hurt my arm, and Officer Jackson kindly offered to bring me home."

"Oh, dear. How bad is it? It's not broken, I hope?"

"No, it's not broken. Just a pulled ligament or two."

"How did it happen?"

"I was trying to throw Officer Jackson over my shoulder, and we sort of fell."

There was a short pause, then her mother asked carefully, "This might be a stupid question, but why would you want to throw a policeman over your shoulder?"

"He was attempting to teach me self-defense at the time," Megan said, beginning to wish she'd made up an excuse.

"Oh, I see." Another pause. "Just who are you planning to defend yourself against?"

Megan sighed. Her mother was the only person in the world who could hold a lengthy conversation consisting entirely of questions. "Don't worry about it, Mom. There won't be any more lessons for a while, in any case."

"Under the circumstances, that might be a good idea. Does your arm hurt? Can you use it?"

Megan flexed the fingers of her injured arm and flinched. "Yes, and no. It's in a sling. I feel pretty ridiculous, to tell the truth."

"Will you be able to manage things by yourself, or do you need some help?"

A crash sounded from the kitchen just then and Megan winced. "I won't be alone, Mom. Officer Jackson will be here for a few days."

"I see." There was a wealth of meaning behind those two words.

"No, Mom, it's not like that. He feels bad because he thinks it was his fault and he wants to help out until my arm is better. He's not going to stay here. I mean, he's not living here or anything—"

She broke off as Tyler's head appeared around the corner. "Sorry about that."

Megan pursed her lips. "What was it?"

"What was what, dear?"

"No, not you, Mom. I was talking to Officer Jackson."

"Tyler," Tyler said impatiently. "I told you to call me Tyler."

"Oh, right. I was talking to Tyler."

"Tyler?"

"The police officer."

"How does a police officer have time to take care of you? Doesn't he have to chase criminals or something?"

"He's giving up his vacation, Mom."

"That's extremely generous of him."

"I'll tell him," Megan said dryly.

"It was a glass thingy," Tyler said, withdrawing his head.

"What glass thingy?" Megan demanded.

"Well, I'd better let you go, dear," her mother said. "You sound as if you are busy. Call me if you need anything."

"I will, Mom. Thanks."

"Come over for dinner. Bring that nice police officer with you."

No way, Megan thought, as she got up to hang up the phone. Tyler had disappeared again. Judging from the sounds coming from the kitchen, he was cleaning up whatever it was he'd dropped. She just hoped it wasn't her new glass mixing bowl.

She sat down again and once more did her best to relax. It wasn't easy. Something told her things were about to get worse. "Are you all right in there?" she called out. "Do you need any help?"

"No! Stay where you are!"

Megan frowned. She'd detected a hint of panic in those words. It took all her willpower to remain on the love seat for the next ten minutes.

She picked up the newspaper she'd left on the coffee table and scanned the front page without any idea what the words said. Since she couldn't open it up with one arm, she let it fall and leaned back with a sigh of frustration.

She longed to get up and find out what Tyler was doing. It drove her crazy having to just sit there and not be able to do anything. She could smell something coming from the kitchen, but couldn't tell what it was. Right then she was hungry enough to eat just about anything, as long as it was edible.

Finally, Tyler poked his head around the corner again. "I'm not sure I did this right."

She frowned at him. "Did what right?"

"Well, it's supposed to be Hamburger Surprise, but it doesn't look like the picture in the cookbook."

"They never do." Megan got off the love seat. "Where is it?"

"On the stove." He looked a little worried. "Don't get upset at the mess. I'll clean up afterward."

She braced herself, walked around the corner into

the kitchen and uttered a shocked yelp. It looked as if he'd sprayed the entire kitchen in tomato juice. Jagged pieces of her new mixing bowl stood on the counter, and it looked as if he'd used every dish in her cupboard.

Grimly keeping her seething thoughts to herself, she picked her way through the mess and peered at the steaming skillet on the stove. Burned hamburger caked the sides of the pan, while a bright orange mess bubbled merrily around lumps of pinkish ground beef. "What did you put in it?" she asked faintly.

"Everything the book said." Tyler glared at the mess in the pan. "I don't know what happened."

Megan peered at the smeared page of her cookbook. "What did you do after you browned the hamburger?"

He shrugged. "I wasn't sure what that meant, so I just threw it all in together."

Don't scream at him, Megan urged herself. She took a long breath. "Tyler, if the recipe had called for everything to be thrown in together, it would have said to throw it all in together. See these instructions down here? That's what you should have followed. Step by step."

Tyler scowled. "Seems like a waste of time to me."

Doing her best to ignore that, she picked up the wooden spoon in her left hand, dipped it into the stuff in the pan, then gingerly touched it to her tongue. Her entire body shuddered at the taste. Very carefully, she laid down the spoon again.

"Just how many meals have you cooked yourself?" she asked sweetly.

Tyler avoided her gaze. "Some. A few."

She waited in grim silence.

"All right! None!" He waved his hand in the air.

"How tough can it be? You just follow recipes in a book. Someone told me that."

"Someone should have told you that there's a little more to it than that."

"Well, how was I to know? That's the first time I've ever seen a cookbook."

"I thought so. What do you usually eat?"

He looked down at his feet. "Fast food, mostly."

"Right. Come here." Megan marched out of the kitchen and walked over to the phone. She waited until he reached her. "Dial this number." She gave him the number then waited while he dialed.

"Who am I dialing?" he asked, lifting the phone to his ear.

"The Pizza Shop. Make it a large one, half pepperoni, half ham and pineapple."

His eyes narrowed dangerously, but he did as she asked. "Thirty minutes," he said briefly, as he hung up the phone. "I'll clean up while we're waiting."

This time she didn't argue with him. She sat on the love seat, forcing herself to calm down. This was not going to work. She'd have to tell him, as kindly as possible, that her nerves couldn't take one more day of this, much less ten.

The doorbell rang a minute or two later, and she started to get up, but Tyler rushed out of the kitchen and waved at her to sit down. "I'll get it. That was fast."

He opened the door, spoke rapidly to whomever stood there, then looked back at her over his shoulder. "Your car's here. I'm just going to run Mike back to his car. Don't move until I get back."

She nodded, wondering what she would do if the pizza arrived before he got back.

She needn't have worried. He must have broken all speed records, as he arrived back before the pizza. She wondered if he'd used his lights and siren, but thought better about asking him.

In any case the pizza arrived just seconds after he returned. He paid for it at the door, and carried it into the kitchen.

It smelled heavenly to Megan, who by now was starving. Tyler insisted that they eat in the living room in front of the television. Remembering the messy kitchen Megan was only too happy to go along with that idea.

Tyler asked her about her job as they were sharing the pizza. She enjoyed telling him about the different places she'd visited, and didn't realize until the meal was over that she'd done all the talking, while Tyler had done all the listening. Although he'd seemed interested enough, she wondered if he'd engineered things that way on purpose. He certainly didn't seem to want to talk about himself.

"I owe you for half of the pizza," Megan said, looking around for her purse as Tyler got up to take the empty box into the kitchen.

"No, that's on me. You can buy the next one."

If he thought they were going to live on a steady diet of pizza, Megan thought grimly, he was in for a big disappointment.

He came back a few minutes later and sat down heavily in the armchair. "It's all cleaned up. I'll replace the bowl tomorrow."

He looked tired, and she felt compelled to say, "That isn't necessary."

"Yes, it is. I'll need it tomorrow."

Megan felt a pang of conscience. "Well, as a matter

of fact, I was thinking about that. I think it might be better—"

"I'll make out a shopping list and go to the store first thing. Tell me what you like to eat and I'll cook it for you."

A vision of her messy kitchen hovered in Megan's mind. "Tyler, I think I'll be able to manage by myself."

His scowl deepened. "There's no way you can manage by yourself. We've been through all that."

"I don't want to be an imposition—"

He lifted his hand to silence her. "I've arranged to take the next two weeks off. I've cleared it with my captain and it's all settled. So stop worrying about it."

He looked so determined, and so sure he was doing the right thing, she couldn't find the words to tell him she'd rather be on her own. It looked like she was stuck with him. That didn't mean she had to put up with his terrible cooking.

"I have a proposition for you," she said, hoping desperately he'd agree.

He gave her a look full of suspicion. "What kind of proposition?"

"I'll show you how to cook in exchange for the self-defense lessons."

"You still want me to teach you self-defense?"

"Of course. Once my arm heals, that is."

He seemed to consider that. "I guess it wouldn't hurt to learn a bit more about cooking," he said at last.

It would help considerably, Megan thought, if it meant they could eat the food. Wisely she kept that comment to herself. "Great. I'll make out a shopping list and we'll plan the meals for the week. That way we won't have to keep going back to the store."

"You don't have to come to the store with me. I can find my way around a grocery store. I've been shopping for myself for six years now."

"What did you do before that?" The question popped out before she realized it.

His face darkened. "I was married. To the wrong woman. I'm not about to make that mistake again."

His tone and the expression on his face warned her he didn't want to discuss it. Nevertheless, she couldn't help saying, "You should have waited until you heard bells."

He looked at her as if she'd said something crazy. "Bells?"

"Bells." She smiled at him. "That's what I'm waiting for. I'm not going to marry any man unless he can make me hear bells when he kisses me."

Tyler shook his head. "Then you might just as well resign yourself to a long, lonely life. The only bells you're gonna hear is in the movies."

He leaned back in his chair and pressed a thumb and forefinger into his eyes in a gesture of weariness. She watched him, wondering again what it was that had made him so cynical.

His bad marriage, no doubt. She was dying to ask him about that, but knew she'd be crossing the line if she did. He was so prickly, he'd probably jump right down her throat.

She couldn't just sit there in silence, however, and he seemed to have run out of conversation. Casting around for a topic, she said tentatively, "I don't suppose you've heard anything about my stolen purse?"

He lowered his hand and gave her a tired look. "Not a thing. I really didn't expect to get it back. I'm sorry."

"So am I. I had some photos in there that are irreplaceable."

"Boyfriend?"

Something about the way he said it made her cringe. He was still treating her like a child. He couldn't be that much older than her, she thought crossly. "I don't keep photos of the men I date," she said, a sharp note in her voice.

His eyes were guarded when he looked at her. "Probably a wise move."

"They were pictures of my brothers and sisters when we were kids."

"You come from a big family?"

"There are five of us. I'm the eldest."

His pensive gaze rested on her face and she knew what he was thinking.

"My youngest brother lives at home with my mother. He's still in high school," she explained. "My two sisters are both working full-time, and my older brother is in the navy. None of them could have taken care of this." She tapped her injured arm.

"I can see that. I'm just glad I could take the time off to do it."

"I'm quite sure there are better things you could do with your vacation time."

"Vacations aren't much fun when you're on your own."

"You don't have friends to go with? Like camping, or hunting with the guys?"

"Cops don't have too many friends."

She felt a pang of sympathy. "You have a tough job. You must want to get away from it sometimes."

His smile was bitter. "You never get away from it. No matter where you are."

Deciding she was on a safe topic, she pursued the subject. "What made you decide to join the police force?"

"A lot of things. A need to see justice done, for the most part, I guess. Too many people get away with murder these days. Literally. Though sometimes I wonder if it's really worth the hassle."

She softened her tone. "You wouldn't be a cop if you really thought that."

"I guess not." He looked at her with a thoughtful expression on his face. "Most of us just want to know we're doing a good job, that's all."

"It must be hard, knowing you're putting your life in danger when you go out on a call."

He shrugged. "I don't think about it, most of the time. My mind is usually too busy figuring out how to handle the situation."

"I saw your citations on the wall at the police station."

"Oh, those." He dismissed them with a brief shake of his head. "They give those things out to everyone."

"I don't think so." She thought about the young, proud, smiling cop in the picture and felt sad. His experiences had hardened and embittered him. She wished there was something she could do about that.

Maybe if she could get him to talk about it, she thought, it might help to release some of that pent-up resentment. She was glad now that she hadn't sent him away. He needed someone to confide in, and it didn't seem as if he had anyone else.

She felt warm inside at the thought of him confiding in her. It had been a long time since anyone had needed her. It was a nice feeling. Now if he could just drop that annoying habit of ordering her around, and quit messing up her kitchen, this situation could turn out to be a lot more pleasant than she'd anticipated.

"Well, I don't know about you," Tyler said, giving an exaggerated yawn, "but I've had a long day. I think it's time I went home."

Megan glanced at her wall clock, surprised by the late hour. "I didn't realize it was so late. Now that I think about it, I guess I am pretty tired."

"Yes, you'd better get to bed. I'll get you settled, then I'll leave."

She froze, praying he didn't mean what she thought he meant. "Settled?" she asked faintly.

He avoided her gaze by staring at the blank screen of the television set. "You're going to need help getting undressed and in bed."

"No," Megan said firmly, "I am not. I can manage really well on my own. I promise you."

"I can't leave until I know you are safely in bed."

He had that stubborn look on his face again. Megan pulled in a slow breath. "I appreciate the offer, Tyler, but I would rather do this myself."

"You could aggravate your injury if you try it on your own. I can't let you do that. Remember what the doctor said. You could do some permanent damage to it."

"Tyler—"

"Look!" He glared at her for an instant and looked away again. "I'm a cop. I've seen just about everything in my job. I've helped deliver babies. I've arrested naked women. I've seen things that would turn your hair white. It's no different from being a doctor."

It was a lot different, Megan thought, beginning to panic. In the first place, she'd never had a doctor who looked like Tyler Jackson. In the second place, she wasn't having a baby or breaking the law. In the third place, for some weird reason she couldn't explain, she found him attractive, which put the whole situation on a different level.

She'd planned on having a shower before she went to bed. Now that didn't seem like such a good idea. "What if I undress myself and get into bed, while you wait out here? Then I'll yell out that I'm okay and you can leave." She could always shower after he'd gone, she thought hopefully.

He got up from the chair slowly, as if he really didn't want to leave it. "You're not listening. You have to get out of those clothes using one arm, and I'm going to see that you do it. So let's go."

"You don't trust me, is that it?"

His mouth tightened. "It's got nothing to do with trust. I want to be right there in case you get stuck, or overbalance or something and need another hand. I'll keep my eyes shut the whole damn time if it will make you feel better, but I'm staying until you are in that bed and settled for the night."

"Why don't you just shower with me while you're about it," she said sweetly.

His eyes narrowed to pale blue slits. "I'll do that, too, if I have to."

"In your dreams. On second thought, maybe this whole idea was a big mistake. Just leave. I'll go stay with my mother."

"Fine. I'll take you. Let's go."

She glared at him, seething with frustration. He knew perfectly well she wasn't about to go clear across town at this time of night to stay with her mother. "You know, you can be really infuriating at times," she muttered.

"So I've been told." He held out his hand in the direction of the hallway. "Lead the way."

"And if I don't?"

"Then we stand here all night arguing about it."

There was nothing else she could say or do to change his mind. In any case, she was much too tired to call his bluff. She turned and headed for the bathroom, praying she could get through this without embarrassing herself too much in the process.

Chapter Four

Her only consolation, Megan thought in exasperation, was that Tyler seemed just as uncomfortable with the situation as she was. He turned on the shower for her, helped her unwrap her arm, then waited outside the bathroom door with his back to her while she undressed.

It was awkward, but she managed. She scrambled into the shower as fast as she could, and stuck her head under the cascading water with a sigh of relief. So far, so good.

Washing her hair with one hand was such a pain she almost asked him for help, but at last she had it clean and rinsed. She turned off the water, then reached a hand around the edge of the shower curtain, groping for the towel.

He must have been waiting for her. The towel was thrust into her hand, and he said gruffly, "I'll be at the door if you need me."

Unnerved by this encounter, she dried herself as best

she could then wrapped the towel around her body before stepping out of the shower. He stood outside the door again, and with a surge of relief she pulled on her nightgown and robe. She couldn't manage the belt and had to leave it unfastened.

Water dripped from her hair, and she rubbed the towel over it with one hand. The cap on the toothpaste refused to come off, no matter how hard she wrestled with it in her teeth. Finally accepting defeat she said grudgingly, "I can't get this off."

He took care not to look at her when he took the toothpaste from her hand and unscrewed the cap. He held out his hand for the toothbrush and she handed it to him, furious with herself for being so helpless. If her arm didn't ache so much, she thought rebelliously, she'd darn well use it and take her chances with it.

Tyler's hand shook slightly as he squeezed toothpaste on the brush, making a squiggly pattern on the bristles.

He wasn't as cool and composed as he pretended to be, Megan thought with satisfaction. She attacked her teeth ferociously, and rinsed the brush under the faucet before replacing it in its holder.

"Your hair is still wet," Tyler remarked unnecessarily.

"I always go to bed with it damp."

"Not that damp. Where's your hair dryer?"

"I'll get it."

"I can do it. Just tell me where."

Too tired to argue with him anymore, she pointed at the cupboard beneath the sink.

It was a weird sensation to stand there while he directed the hot blast of air at her hair. She closed her eyes and tried to forget she was standing half-undressed in her bathroom with a cop she hardly knew.

When her hair was dry he picked up the bottle of painkillers and shook one out into his palm. She watched him fill a glass half-full with water, and took it from him when he handed it to her.

"I have to wrap your arm again," he said gruffly, when she'd swallowed the tiny pill.

She sat on the edge of bed in silence while he bandaged her arm, trying not to flinch every time his warm fingers brushed her bare skin. She thanked him in a cool, polite voice when he was finally done.

"Don't get out of that bed until I get here in the morning," he ordered, as he straightened up. "I'll be back around seven. I've still got your key so I'll let myself in."

"Don't rush on my account."

A gleam appeared in his eye but he ignored the wry comment. Now that she was ready for bed he seemed in a hurry to leave. "Sleep well," he said, "and watch you don't lie on that arm."

"I'll do my best." She gave him a pleasant smile and held it until she heard the front door close with a decisive thud. Then she let out a loud groan and fell back on the bed. That had been the most embarrassing ordeal of her life. And it was only the beginning.

Heaven knew what was in store for her the next ten days. If they both managed to survive without killing each other it would be nothing short of a miracle.

Outside the apartment, Tyler rolled down the windows of his car to allow the cool night air to flow gently over his heated brow. He was not a happy man.

That whole scenario in there had made him sweat. Being that close to Megan Summers's half-clad body in the intimacy of her bedroom had proved to be far more disrupting to his nerves than he'd anticipated.

One whiff of that exotic fragrance that had followed her out of the shower and all his good intentions had vanished in a puff of smoke. Everything about her tormented him—the way she moved, the sound of her voice sending ripples over his skin, the flash of fire in her green eyes when she was mad at him.

Which was a lot, he thought with a wry grimace. Not that he could blame her after messing up her kitchen. Not to mention breaking that bowl. Cooking was a lot tougher than it looked. Which was probably why he never cooked for himself.

This whole idea was beginning to look like a disaster. Tyler leaned back and closed his eyes. If he had any sense he'd take her right over to her mother's house in the morning. Except that he wasn't sure her mother would be diligent enough to make sure her daughter didn't use that arm.

There was no doubt in Tyler's mind that Megan needed watching. Megan Summers was definitely the most independent, stubborn, self-willed woman he'd been around in years. She would need monitoring all the time to make sure she didn't disobey the doctor's orders and screw up her arm for good.

Tyler wasn't about to let that happen. He'd caused the injury in the first place, and if she permanently damaged her arm he'd have that on his conscience for the rest of his life.

He was going to make darn sure that she got all the help she needed until the arm was healed, and he would just have to do his best to ignore what she did to his hormones.

He leaned forward and started the engine, praying that he had enough self-control to keep that resolution.

That night was a long one for Tyler. He slept badly, waking up out of nightmares that had nothing to do with Megan and everything to do with his conscience. He was glad when the morning came so he had an excuse to get up.

A few miles away Megan was also thinking about getting up. She'd woken up twice in the night, her throbbing arm preventing her from going back to sleep right away. By the time daylight had filtered through the blinds, she'd had enough of tossing around in the bed.

Her alarm clock showed 6:15 a.m. on the dial. Forty-five minutes or so before Tyler was due to arrive. Just enough time to get into some clothes and attempt to do something with her hair.

Getting dressed proved to be a lot more difficult than the reverse procedure. She'd managed to undo her bra fairly easily the night before. Doing one up with one hand proved to be an impossibility.

She sank on the bed and considered the choices. She could go without a bra, of course. The idea had never appealed to her, and considering the circumstances, it seemed like a bad idea right now.

She could struggle into it as best she could, then wait for Tyler to arrive to fasten it for her. She frowned, chewing her lip. That was just slightly better than looking for a female neighbor to help her. Maybe she should have stayed with her mother, after all.

She was almost tempted to call her and ask if she could stay there. But then she'd have to put up with her mother's endless questions, her constant comments about her eldest daughter's lack of marriage plans, hints about grandchildren and the dire warnings that Megan's biological clock was about to run out.

There were definite disadvantages to being the eldest in the family, Megan thought, gazing balefully at the phone. All in all, she'd rather take her chances with Officer Jackson.

That having been decided, she got as far into her bra as she could manage, pulled on a pair of khaki cotton pants, which meant struggling with the zipper for a full minute and a half, then dragged a yellow cotton sweater off its hanger and tugged it over her head. She managed to call her office by wedging the receiver in her shoulder while she dialed. After explaining her predicament and promising to be back as soon as her arm healed, she replaced the receiver with a sigh of relief.

The whole procedure had taken far longer than she'd expected. She'd barely paid a visit to the bathroom before she heard the key in the lock of her front door.

She stared at Tyler as he walked into her living room. Tyler Jackson in tight jeans was something to stare at. No one would ever think he was a cop, she thought, taking in his dark blue polo shirt and sneakers. Not that she knew that many cops with whom she could compare him.

He scowled at her when he saw her standing there. "I thought I told you to stay in bed," he said, dropping the small sack he was carrying onto the coffee table. "I hope you didn't use that arm. How is it? Does it still hurt? Isn't it supposed to be in the sling?"

Megan sighed. He was beginning to sound more like her mother all the time. "I got up because nature called," she said pointedly.

"You could have gone back to bed."

"It didn't seem worth it once I'd gone through all the trouble of getting in and out of the bathroom."

"You didn't have to get dressed."

"I didn't entirely." Abandoning all sense of propriety, she turned her back on him and lifted the hem of her sweater. "I need help with my bra."

She waited for what seemed an eternity for him to move. Finally, after a lengthy silence that made her nerves squeeze tight, he cleared his throat.

His fingers touched her bare back and she jumped, then silently cursed herself for reacting so childishly.

"Sorry," he muttered. "It's been a long time since I did this."

She started wondering whose bra he used to do up, then made herself stop wondering. She tried to breathe evenly while his fingers fumbled with the catch. After several agonizing moments she heard him breathe a sigh of relief. "There. Got it."

"Thank you." It was a little difficult to sound dignified as she pulled her sweater down, but she managed it.

"Now, where's that sling?"

"Still in the bathroom. I'll get it."

"I'll get it. You sit down."

"I keep telling you, there's nothing wrong with my legs." She started back across the room. "I need to keep walking around or I'll start getting weak."

When she came back from the bathroom he was in the kitchen, pouring water into the coffeepot.

"I brought doughnuts for breakfast," he said, deftly measuring coffee into the basket. "I thought it would be easier."

Megan briefly closed her eyes in resignation and mentally gave up her planned breakfast of cereal and fruit. "I'll make a shopping list," she said, as she reached for a couple of mugs from the cupboard. "We can go to the store this morning."

She tried not to notice the smears of tomato juice on the counter or the small, dried orange puddle on the floor. She'd just have to get to it later, she promised herself.

"Let me fix that sling before you do anything else," Tyler said, picking it up from the back of the chair where she'd draped it.

Once more she bore the sweet agony of his fingers fumbling at the back of her neck. After assuring him the sling was comfortable, she concentrated on putting the doughnuts on a plate.

It had been years since she'd eaten doughnuts for breakfast. She'd forgotten how good they tasted, she thought, as she sat across from Tyler at her small dinette table. With someone like Tyler Jackson around she'd soon get into bad habits.

He'd propped the newspaper against the coffeepot and was reading her snippets of news. He really did have a great voice, she decided. The sort of lazy, husky drawl that seemed to worm its way into her skin. He read very well, stopping now and then to make a comment or shake his head over something in the news that bothered him.

She took the opportunity to really study him, and decided that he wasn't really handsome, yet he had the kind of indefinable charisma that most women adored. His rugged jaw had been freshly shaved, and his chiseled face and piercing blue eyes gave him a streetwise look that appealed to her adventurous nature.

She liked the way his dark hair fell across his forehead, making him look almost boyish, in direct contrast to the harsh frown that constantly lurked on his face.

He was not the most sociable of beings, judging from some of his comments. Yet she couldn't help feeling that somewhere behind that wall of reserve the young, smiling cop in the picture waited for the chance to reemerge. All he really needed was for someone to understand him.

She longed to know what had gone wrong with his life. Why he was no longer married, and what it was that had made him so excessively vigilant.

He looked up suddenly, taking her by surprise. His expression changed when he realized she'd been staring at him. "If you've got that list ready I'll go to the store," he said, getting up abruptly from his chair.

"I'm coming, too." She finished the last gulp of her coffee and pushed her chair back.

"I'd rather go on my own."

"I know you would, but I'm coming anyway. I'll go crazy sitting around here with nothing to do."

"You could watch TV."

She gave him a look that she hoped conveyed her contempt for that idea. "You'll have to write the list while I dictate."

"Right." He gave her a sharp scrutiny. "How was your arm last night? Did it bother you?"

She shrugged. "Some. I took a pill when I got up, though, so it feels better now."

He seemed satisfied with that, and she silently thanked heaven that he didn't ask her about the toothpaste. She'd had to hold the tube down with her injured hand while she took off the cap. If he'd known about that she'd have been in for another patronizing lecture.

He seemed preoccupied on the way to the store, and

she wondered if he was worrying about something. She was about to ask him when he said abruptly, "I think your mother might have the wrong idea about me."

Wondering where that came from, Megan said carefully, "My mother gets the wrong idea about everyone I meet. Don't let it throw you. She's under the mistaken impression that I would be better off married than living alone." She almost added that her mother's anxiety stemmed from an intense longing to have grandchildren, but she thought better of it.

He glanced at her, the familiar frown creasing his brow. "I don't want to ruin your reputation."

He sounded so old-fashioned she almost laughed out loud. "I didn't know there was such a thing anymore."

He looked uncomfortable. "You know what I mean. I wouldn't want anyone to think that we're…"

"Romantically involved?" she prodded gently.

"That's one way of putting it." He frowned through the windshield at the road ahead.

"What way would you put it?" a little demon made her ask.

"I don't want anyone to think we're sleeping together."

His words produced a quiver of awareness that she quickly suppressed. "I really don't think that's anyone's business."

"Some people make it their business."

"Well, you can stop worrying about my mother. She trusts me to be sensible about these things."

He shot her a glance and said in his patronizing parent voice, "I'm glad to hear it."

Megan resisted the temptation to pull a face at him.

The shopping trip went quite well, all things considered. The first thing Tyler bought was a new mixing bowl, which Megan really appreciated. After that he eyed just about everything she bought with suspicion, but refrained from commenting too much. He did mutter something about the alfalfa sprouts looking like weeds, and Megan guessed that he wasn't too well informed about nutritious foods.

He turned up his nose when she asked him if he liked yogurt and told her he didn't care much for vegetables, which made her all the more determined to teach him how to cook a decent meal.

His favorite foods, it seemed, were ice cream and frozen French fries. He seemed put out when Megan bought sherbet instead of ice cream and frowned when she absolutely refused to buy the fries.

"I like fries with my meals," he told her, opening the freezer case door.

She closed it again before he had a chance to reach in. "A baked potato is much better for you."

"I don't like baked potatoes." He opened the door again.

"You'll like mine." She closed it again. "I don't have room in my freezer for all that frozen stuff. In any case, cooking fresh products is more nutritious."

He gave her a dark look. "No wonder you're so slim," he grumbled. "What about beer? Or are you going to tell me that's bad for me, too?"

"That's bad for you, too."

"Figures." He picked up a couple of six-packs and dropped them into the basket. "If you're going to make me eat like a rabbit, I'm going to need a couple of beers to keep up my strength."

If things were left to him, she thought darkly, as they waited in line at the checkout, she'd put on ten pounds in a week and raise her cholesterol to an unacceptable level. It amazed her that he could stay in such great shape if he ate all that junk food.

He argued with her when she insisted on paying for the groceries, but relented when she told him he could pay for the mixing bowl.

Outside in the parking lot, she watched him toss the heavy sacks into the trunk of the car as if they were full of tissue paper instead of groceries. He had thrown her just as easily over his shoulder the other night. Just the memory of it made shivers run down her back. In which case, she hastily told herself, she'd better stop thinking about it.

He climbed in beside her and turned the key in the ignition. "Anywhere else you need to go before we go home?"

"I don't think so."

"How's the arm?"

"Aching."

He pulled out of the parking lot and drove toward the apartment building. "Isn't it time for another painkiller?"

She sighed. He was driving her crazy. That's all she needed—another solicitous parent to contend with. "I'll take another pill when we get home."

"See that you do."

"Right, sir."

He glanced at her out of the corner of his eye. "Sarcasm doesn't suit you."

"Neither does dictatorship."

He looked offended, and she immediately felt sorry.

"I'm only trying to do what's best for you," he said huffily.

"I know." She hesitated. "I do appreciate it, Tyler,

but do you think you could do it without sounding like my father?"

He seemed surprised at that. He shot her a look that she couldn't quite define. "Believe me," he said, with just a hint of irony in his voice, "I don't feel in the least like your father."

She wasn't quite sure how to take that. She was tempted to ask him who he did feel like, but thought better of it. He might think she was trying to be provocative, and she didn't want him getting the wrong idea.

She might find the man attractive, she assured herself, but there was no way she could get serious about a man who ordered her around as if she were one of his subordinates in the police force. Or worse, his kid sister.

Tyler insisted on putting all the groceries away, while she told him where everything went. By the time that was accomplished, it was time to start thinking about lunch.

She got by that one by suggesting soup and salad, and hunks of French bread to go with it. "I'll get the stuff for the salad," she announced, opening the door of the fridge.

"No, I'll get it." He nudged her gently out of the way with his shoulder.

The contact sent a delicious shudder down the affected arm. Unnerved by the sensation, she moved out of his way and opened the cupboard containing her pots and pans.

The one she wanted rested on the top of the pile, and she reached for it. As she straightened, Tyler snaked his hand around from behind her and closed his hand over hers.

"I'll take that."

His voice had sounded right in her ear. Combined with the pressure of his fingers, she felt the impact all the way down to her toes.

She spun around to face him, meaning to hand him the saucepan, but something in his expression froze her. Seconds ticked by while he just stood there, inches away, staring into her eyes with a hungry look on his face.

She could feel her heart thumping, and a weird sensation as if she were dropping through space at high speed. Then his expression changed, and he cleared his throat.

"This is my job," he said, taking the saucepan out of her nerveless fingers.

She was too shaken to resist. She must have imagined it, she told herself, as she moved away from him. Yet the image of that intense look on his face stayed with her as she watched him wash the lettuce.

"Okay, I can manage now," he told her, after he'd opened the soup and poured it into the pan. "Go and sit down in there and I'll yell when it's ready."

"You still have to slice tomatoes for the salad." Needing something to do, she lit the gas under the soup. "I'll watch the soup while you do that."

"No, you won't. You'll go sit down like I told you and read the paper, or watch TV or something."

She frowned at him. "You're doing it again."

"I'm doing what's best for you."

"You're ordering me around."

"And you're being stubborn. This is a simple meal. A child could handle it. Now go sit down. You look tired."

Without another word she left him and stalked into

the living room. Tired. That's what every woman wanted to hear. Not that it mattered to her what he thought of her, of course.

She stared at the front page of the newspaper. If they were going to get through this week with any kind of peace she would have to make him realize that just because her arm was out of action she wasn't totally disabled. He had to stop regarding her as an accident waiting to happen.

And she had to stop jumping every time he looked at her or touched her. Even now she was getting a shivery feeling just thinking about it. Annoyed with herself, she tried to concentrate on the headline story.

"Damn!"

The hoarse curse rang out in the kitchen sometime later and brought her to her feet. "What's the matter?"

"Nothing. Just stay there. Everything's fine."

Megan sniffed. everything didn't smell fine. Cautiously she edged around the corner and peered into the kitchen.

Smoke hovered over the stove, while Tyler furiously mopped up the bubbling soup that ran down the front of the oven. She opened her mouth to comment but just then the smoke alarm went off with a shrill buzz that seemed to vibrate right through her head.

"Damn," Tyler said again, giving her a desperate look. He raised his voice to be heard above the alarm. "The soup boiled over when I wasn't looking."

"Really. Well, if you remember, I did offer to watch it for you."

He gave her a look that would have stopped Attila the Hun. "I was busy making salad. My mind was on other things."

"Well, you'd better turn off that alarm before the fire department turns up."

"Where is it?"

"In the hallway!" She waved her good arm in that direction. "Just follow your ears."

He grabbed a kitchen towel and plunged by her, and a few seconds later blessed peace was restored.

She waited for him to come back, resisting the urge to pick up the cloth and finish mopping the stove. This was it, she thought, surveying the mess. From now on she was through following his orders.

He was going to learn to cook a decent meal if she had to stand over him and supervise each step. But there was no way she was going to let him loose on his own in her kitchen again.

Tyler was quieter than usual as they shared the meal later. If only he would let her help, things would be easier for both of them. There was plenty she could do with her good arm, if only he'd quit babying her.

Looking at his gloomy expression, she decided he needed cheering up. "The salad's good," she said brightly, as she laid down her fork.

"Uh-huh."

"So's the soup."

He looked at her with narrowed eyes. "I manage to cook soup all the time at home. It's easier to concentrate when I'm on my own."

Now who was being defensive, she thought. Determined not to enter into another argument, she searched around for another topic. "Have you always lived in Portland?" she asked finally.

"Nope." He broke off a chunk of bread and took a bite.

She waited, and when nothing else appeared to be

forthcoming prompted, "Where did you live before you came here?"

"Southern Oregon." He flicked a glance her way then went back to cleaning his soup plate with the rest of his bread.

"Was that when you were married?"

The hand holding the bread stilled, then moved on. "As a matter of fact it was."

Obviously it was still painful for him. "I'm sorry," she said quietly. "It's none of my business. I shouldn't have brought it up."

This time his silver-blue gaze remained on her face. "It's no big deal. It was over a long time ago."

She nodded, wondering if she dared say any more.

She was still trying to form a question in her mind when he added, "Six years ago, in fact. I transferred to Portland right after that."

"I'm sorry. That must have been dismal."

He popped the last piece of bread in his mouth and swallowed it down before answering her. "The whole damn thing was dismal. Lousy marriages always are." He got up from the table, taking the plates with him, and went into the kitchen.

Megan waited until she heard the water running into the sink, then followed him in there. He stood with his back to her, but she had hardly gone three steps before he said sharply, "Go sit down. I'll be through here in a minute."

"I'd really like to help." She reached his side and opened up the dishwasher. "I can stack with one hand."

For once he didn't argue. In fact, she felt a little worried about him. He seemed deep in thought over something. She hoped she hadn't brought back any bad memories.

On the other hand, she thought, as she stacked the plates into the dishwasher, if he could only open up and talk about it, he might be able to lay to rest whatever ghosts were troubling him.

It didn't seem likely he would talk about it with her, however, and maybe she should just quit trying. They found enough to argue about without bringing his broken marriage into it.

She was pleasantly surprised when they managed to get through the entire afternoon on amicable terms. She'd suggested working on a jigsaw puzzle together, something she could do with one hand, and Tyler readily agreed. He seemed relieved to have something to concentrate his attention on.

He was good at it, and she had a hard time keeping up with him. The afternoon passed quickly, while they exchanged views on several topics, including a lively discussion on the merits of the city's use of police on horseback, the concept of which Megan heartily approved, while Tyler felt it was a waste of taxpayer's money.

Much as she would have liked to, however, Megan could not steer the conversation in a personal direction, and by dinnertime she knew no more about Tyler's background than the little he'd already told her.

He made her sit on a chair in the kitchen while he prepared the evening meal. She supervised each step, and in spite of a couple of mishaps while breaking eggs into the bowl, he managed to make a pretty good meat loaf.

She insisted on helping with the dishes afterward, stacking them into the dishwasher for him. Tyler was looking pretty pleased with himself when they returned to the living room.

"I'll have to remember that recipe," he said, as he settled himself into an armchair. "Maybe I could cook it for myself now and again."

"I'll give you the recipe," Megan said, mentally deciding to buy him an entire cookbook. "That's if you promise to follow it faithfully."

"I'll try. I don't have much patience with instructions. I tend to play it by ear."

No kidding, she thought wryly. Maybe she'd taken on more than she'd bargained for when she'd offered to teach him to cook.

Remembering how she'd felt earlier when he'd stared at her in the kitchen, she had to admit that the cooking lessons weren't the only thing she hadn't bargained on. If she wasn't real careful, she warned herself uneasily, she could be in big trouble before this whole thing was over.

Chapter Five

"What do you usually do on a Friday night?" Tyler asked, breaking into Megan's troubled thoughts.

The question took her by surprise. "Sometimes I go out to dinner with friends. Sometimes I go to a movie, if no one else is around."

"You go alone?" He frowned. "That's not a very bright idea."

She felt a faint prickle of resentment and did her best to ignore it. "It's perfectly safe. There are plenty of other people around. It's not as if I'm on my own. What can happen in a movie theater?"

"Plenty. You'd be surprised. What about the parking lot? You walk to your car alone in the dark, right?"

"There are other people around there, too."

"Exactly. What would you do if some guy came up behind you and stuck a gun in your back?"

"Scream like the blazes," Megan said promptly.

"There aren't too many people around who would

argue with a gun. He could force you into your car and you wouldn't be able to do a thing about it."

"I'd fight," Megan said, lifting her chin.

"I wouldn't recommend it. He's liable to shoot you just to keep you quiet."

"What about the self-defense lessons? Isn't that what they are for?"

Tyler shook his head. "If you hadn't hurt yourself that night I would have given you the lecture about not fighting a man with a gun. You only use self-defense if you are reasonably sure it will work. Competing with a firearm is a losing proposition."

"Then what good are the lessons?"

"We hope to give you an edge. We don't guarantee complete immunity from harm. In certain circumstances a thorough knowledge of self-defense could save your life. That doesn't necessarily mean it will. The only way you can be reasonably safe is if you behave sensibly. And that means not going to places alone where there could be trouble."

Aware that she was being lectured again, Megan dug in her heels. "Well, I'm not going to let my life be dictated by what might possibly happen. If I do that then the bad guys win. I'm going to live my life the way I want, and no one, with or without a gun, is going to stop me doing that."

"I'll make sure they put that on your gravestone," Tyler said, looking perfectly serious. "It's attitudes like yours that make our job so tough."

"Really. I was under the impression that it was criminals who did that."

He waved an impatient hand at her. "You know what I mean."

"Of course. You're insinuating that I'm not mature enough or sensible enough to take care of myself."

"That's got nothing to do with it." He sat up, apparently warming up to what was obviously a hot topic for him. "I'm saying that most women do not understand how vulnerable they really are. What with the increasing availability of drugs and firearms, the world has become a dangerous place. Violence is everywhere and anywhere, and women in particular are at the mercy of these vicious thugs."

"I know," Megan murmured facetiously. "It's a jungle out there."

He scowled at her. "It's no joke. I tried to tell my wife that, but she wouldn't listen, either."

Megan's resentment vanished in a flash. She held her breath, almost afraid to hear what he had to say next. Maybe now she'd find out exactly what did happen to Tyler's marriage. Only now she wasn't sure she wanted to know.

"We ended up getting a divorce." Tyler leaned back and massaged his brow with his thumb and forefinger.

Relieved that things hadn't turned out as tragic as she'd imagined, Megan said quietly, "I'm sorry."

"I knew it was coming. Katy had always been very independent. She didn't like anyone telling her what to do. Especially me."

Megan thought about the way Tyler barked out orders and felt a pang of sympathy for Katy. "Did you have children?"

"No, thank God. She was too busy with her career."

"What does she do?"

"She works for the D.A.'s office. That's how we met. We were both lonely, I guess, and kind of drifted into a relationship. Getting married seemed like a good idea at the time."

So far he hadn't mentioned anything about love, Megan thought. "How long were you married?"

Tyler sighed. "Too long. It was a disaster right from the start. I was working nights a lot, and Katy got tired of sitting at home. She started going out, visiting her parents at first, then out with her friends. She didn't understand that I needed to know exactly where she was going and what she was doing. She got mad when I wouldn't let her go places without me. I just wanted to be sure she was safe, that was all. She said I was trying to run her life."

"Didn't you discuss it with her? Try to compromise with each other?"

He uttered a bitter laugh. "You couldn't argue with Katy. She wouldn't listen to reason. She just got mad. Then she'd do something to make me mad, like disappear for hours without telling me where she was, or going somewhere I'd warned her was dangerous to go to alone."

"That must have worried you."

"You bet it worried me. And she knew it. In the end we were arguing just about every night, until finally we both realized we couldn't live with each other any more and agreed to call it quits."

"That's a shame."

He shrugged. "Maybe. All I know is that I did my best to protect her, and she threw it all right back in my face."

"I don't think she meant to do that." She'd more or less spoken her thoughts out loud, and waited apprehensively for his answer.

"Oh, she meant it, all right. If you'd met her, you'd know what I mean."

She should just drop it here, Megan thought. Somehow she just couldn't let it go. "Maybe I didn't know her, but I can understand how she must have felt. I know you wanted to protect her, but everyone needs their own space, Tyler. No one should have to account for every second of her life, no matter what the circumstances are. She probably felt stifled and needed a little freedom, that's all."

"Freedom for what? To live dangerously? Well, if she wanted that, she married the wrong person." He stood up abruptly and looked at his watch. "I don't know why I'm telling you all this, anyway. The last thing you need is a rundown on my sordid past."

"Tyler..." She jumped to her feet, wishing now that she'd kept her thoughts to herself.

"Since you managed to get yourself out of bed," he said a little too quietly, "and into the shower this morning, I figure you can manage without me tonight. My number's in the book if you have any problem."

"Tyler, I'm sorry."

"There's nothing to be sorry about. Forget it." He strode to the door and opened it.

"Will I see you tomorrow?"

He turned and looked at her. "I'll be here to get your breakfast," he said gruffly. "Don't forget to take your pill and don't use that arm."

Before she could answer him he'd stepped outside and closed the door behind him.

Megan sank onto her chair, feeling more miserable than she had any right to feel. She hadn't meant to upset him. All she'd wanted to do was make him understand why his wife had acted the way she had. Of course, it was none of her business and she should have kept her mouth shut.

Remembering what he'd said just before he left, she wondered how he knew she'd showered that morning. Most likely he'd noticed the bandage on her arm was damp. She hadn't taken it off in the shower, aware that she wouldn't be able to put it back on by herself.

She looked at the phone and wondered how long it would take him to get home. If he'd gone straight home. In that mood he might have decided to drown his sorrows in some bar. She had a vision of him sitting there, all alone, gazing into his beer with that gloomy expression of his. Her imagination supplied a lonely woman, sidling up to him to keep him company.

The thought made her feel so bad she put it out of her mind at once. Not that it mattered to her how many women Tyler Jackson picked up in a bar. She just didn't like to think she'd driven him there, that was all.

She looked at the clock. It was too early to go to bed, and she didn't feel like finishing the jigsaw puzzle. It just didn't seem as much fun without Tyler. There was nothing on television she cared to watch, and she didn't feel like reading.

The evening seemed to stretch out endlessly in front of her. She couldn't wait for the morning to come so she could mend her fences with him. But the morning was still a long way away. She glanced at the phone again.

No, she couldn't call him. That might give him the wrong idea. What she needed was something to take her mind off Officer Jackson.

She reached for the phone and tucked it under her chin, then punched out a number. If she couldn't go out with her friends on a Friday night, she told herself, she could at least talk to one of them.

After dialing four numbers, all answered by a machine, she had to acknowledge the fact that all her friends were out enjoying their Friday evening. She was beginning to feel very sorry for herself.

She looked up Tyler's number and scribbled it as best she could with her left hand in her address book. She almost called him, her hand hovering over the phone while she struggled with indecision. At the last minute she dialed her mother's number instead, in a desperate attempt to put the infuriating man out of her mind.

This time, of course, she got an answer.

"Hello, Megan, is something wrong?"

It was amazing how her mother could make her feel guilty without actually saying anything, Megan thought. "Everything's fine, Mom. I do call you just to say hi once in a while, you know."

"I hope this is one of those times?"

Megan sighed. "I'm sitting here all by myself on a Friday night and I wanted someone to talk to, that's all."

"What about that nice police officer? Isn't he staying with you?"

"Not all the time, Mom. I told you, he goes home to his apartment at night."

"I see. How is your arm? Getting better?"

"It's not aching so much, thanks."

"Good. Then why don't you and your police officer come over to dinner tomorrow night."

"Mom, Tyler is not my police officer. I told you—"

"I know what you told me, dear. I would like to

meet him just the same. He must be quite special to give up his vacation to look after you."

Her mother was off on the wrong track as usual. Megan searched in her mind for an excuse why she and Tyler couldn't go to dinner and couldn't think of one. Actually, now that she thought about it, the dinner thing might not be such a bad idea. Once her mother saw the two of them together, she'd realize that there could never be any serious relationship between them. Then maybe she'd quit bugging her daughter about him.

Apart from anything else, it would get her out of the house, Megan decided, and save Tyler from having to struggle with a meal. As long as they were with her mother they wouldn't be able to argue, something that was becoming a habit judging by the last few hours they were together.

"All right," she said, giving in to the impulse. "We'd love to come. What time do you want us, and can we bring anything?"

It felt strange to be linking herself with Tyler that way. Strange and just a little disturbing. Preoccupied with the thought, she missed what her mother had said and had to ask her to repeat it.

She had barely hung up from the call when the phone rang. Her leap of hope made her sound breathless when she spoke her name.

The husky voice that answered her sent shivers up and down her back. "I just wanted you to know that I'm at home," Tyler said.

"I'm glad you called," she said unsteadily. "I appreciate the thought."

"If you need me I can be back there in ten minutes."

She was tempted to say she needed him. Only that,

she was quite sure, would be a big mistake. "I'm fine, Tyler. Please don't worry about me."

There was a long pause at the end of the line, then he said gruffly, "I'll see you in the morning, then. Just be careful with that arm."

"I will." She hung up, feeling as if someone had wrapped a warm blanket around her heart. He'd cared enough to call.

Not that she should read too much into that, she warned herself, as she got ready for bed later. That was just Tyler's way of easing his conscience. She would be very stupid to imagine it meant anything more than that. She would be incredibly stupid to *want* it to mean anything more than that. She and Tyler, she assured herself, would never make it together. They would drive each other crazy in much less time than it took for his first marriage to fail. She'd do well to remember that the next time she felt all cozy and warm at the sight of his rare smile, or at the touch of his fingers brushing her skin.

In spite of her self-lectures, however, it took her what seemed an eternity to fall asleep. It wasn't her aching arm keeping her awake, or even the warm, humid air drifting in the open window. It was the memory of Tyler's voice, telling her he was only ten minutes away.

Tyler's sleep that night was haunted by dreams again. Dreams about his ex-wife, all mixed up with dreams about Megan, until he had the two of them confused. He woke up in a sweat, and with a strange feeling of excitement.

Normally he greeted each morning with a kind of dull resignation, prepared to accept whatever the day might offer. He didn't think much past that. In his job it didn't pay to dwell on the possibilities.

This morning, however, he felt a weird sense of expectation, as if something different were waiting for him just around the corner. He tumbled out of bed, still dazed with sleep and eager to get the day started. He was curious to know what it was that filled him with such a great feeling of anticipation.

It wasn't until he was fully awake that he remembered he wasn't going to work today. He was on vacation, at the beck and call of a certain young woman who managed to raise his blood pressure every time he got within five yards of her.

Tyler peered into the mirror and groaned at his bleary-eyed reflection. He'd offered to be her nursemaid in a rash moment of guilt, and had spent most of the time since regretting his stupidity.

He was in a constant state of turmoil when he was around Megan Summers. She was either arousing his temper or arousing something else, neither of which was too comfortable.

To make matters worse, he found himself telling her things he'd never talked about to anyone else. Things he thought he'd buried a long time ago. She had a way of dredging up his past. He didn't want to remember his past. Most of it was too painful.

His vision blurred a little when he thought about Mason. His brother had depended on him, and he had never been able to escape the feeling that he'd let him down when it mattered the most. Even now, so many years later, he still wished he could talk to Mason and explain why he was helpless to save him.

Tyler shook his head, forcing his mind onto other things. He'd promised to cook breakfast for Megan, and he'd better get over there before she disobeyed him and tried to do it herself.

He arrived at her apartment a little while later. She was listening to the stereo. He could hear the thud of the bass right through the door.

Mindful of walking in on her unexpectedly again, he rang the bell. She didn't answer and after trying a couple of times to get her attention, he gave up and opened the door with the key she'd given him.

She was dancing, waltzing around the room with her good arm outstretched, and the other tucked in at waist level. She was wearing shorts and a sleeveless denim shirt.

Her legs, like her arms, were lightly tanned. He couldn't seem to take his eyes off them as she swept gracefully around the floor.

Suddenly the legs came to an abrupt stop and he heard her gasp. "I wasn't expecting you so early," she said, sounding breathless.

He jerked his gaze to her flushed face and held up the key. "You didn't hear the bell so I let myself in."

"Oh, sorry. I guess it is a little loud. I'll turn it off."

He watched her, mesmerized, as she leaned over to turn off the stereo. Silently cursing, he tore his gaze away from her before his imagination took him to where he wasn't supposed to go.

Several albums lay scattered over the coffee table, he noticed. It looked as if she'd been up for some time. "Have you eaten breakfast yet?" he asked her, as she closed the door.

"No, I've been waiting for you." She walked over to the coffee table and began piling the record albums on top of each other.

"You're not wearing your sling," Tyler said, frowning at her arm. "And where's the bandage?"

"I took it off when I had a shower."

"I'll wrap it again for you. How does it feel?"

"Better. It only hurts now when I use it."

Concern made his voice rise. "You're not supposed to be using your arm."

She gave him a rebellious look. "I'm not using it, exactly. I meant when I touch it."

He wasn't at all sure that was what she meant. He wasn't going to argue with her, but he was going to make damn sure she didn't use her arm while he was around. "I'll get the bandage. Where is it?"

"I'll get it. It's in the bathroom."

By the time she returned, he'd stacked the albums back in their rack.

She stood in silence while he wrapped her arm and tied it in the sling. When he'd finished, she said in a small voice, "Could you please fasten my bra?"

"Sure." The word came out more like a croak. Steeling himself, he fumbled with the catch while he fought the urge to brush his fingers across her bare back. His mouth was dry by the time he was through. Moving away from her abruptly he headed for the kitchen.

"My mother has invited us to dinner tonight," she announced, following behind him.

Shock waves rippled down his spine. He reached for the coffee canister and opened it. "Us?" he repeated carefully.

"Well, actually she invited me," Megan said hastily. "But since I can't drive, she included you in the invitation."

Things were getting too complicated, Tyler thought,

as he measured coffee into the pot. Dinner with her mother sounded just a little too cozy for his liking. What was it Megan had said? *My mother gets the wrong idea about everyone I meet.*

That's all he needed. A mother who suspected something was going on between him and her daughter. The only thing that was going on was in his treacherous mind, but he could hardly tell Megan's mother that. She'd think he was some kind of weird lech.

"You don't have to drive me if you'd rather not," Megan said, sounding deliberately offhand. "I can always get a cab."

Realizing that he'd taken too long to answer her, he said quickly, "Of course I'll drive you. That was part of the deal, right? I was just wondering how your mother might feel having to feed a total stranger."

"My mother likes to cook. She's good at it."

"Then you'd better not mention my feeble efforts." He held the coffeepot under the faucet and filled it to the line with water.

"You're doing just fine for a beginner." Standing alongside of him, she reached up in the cupboard for the mugs.

He tried to ignore the enticing length of her body stretched so close to his arm. He tried not to notice the fragrance that had intrigued him the night she'd come out of the shower. He tried desperately not to imagine her in the shower.

He could remember vividly the feel of her slim waist in his hands, and the feel of her supple body sliding over his shoulder the night of the lessons. His entire nervous system reminded him potently of the sensations he'd felt then.

He swallowed hard, trying to concentrate on something else...anything else that would take his mind away from how much he wanted to hold her again.

This was crazy. He couldn't have the hots for this woman. She was everything he'd spent the last six years doing his best to avoid. She was too independent, too outspoken, too rebellious, too fond of getting her own way.

Forget that she was also intelligent, funny and sexy as hell. Right now he was feeling vulnerable because she needed him. Being needed made him feel good inside, as if in some strange way he was making up for what happened to Mason.

He felt that way whenever he helped out someone in need, and that's all it was with Megan, he told himself as he measured coffee into the pot with grim determination. She needed him, and he needed to be needed. It was as simple as that. Just as soon as her arm was healed, and she was no longer dependent on him, they would go their separate ways.

Well, not quite, he remembered with a jolt. There were still the self-defense lessons. He'd have to find some way of getting out of that deal. There was no way he could wrestle around with her on the mat now. He was likely to lose his cool and forget all the reasons he should stay out of her life.

He was still trying to figure a way out of the lessons as he drove Megan to her mother's apartment early that evening. The need to do so was becoming increasingly necessary. All day long he'd been tortured by the urge to take her in his arms and kiss her until she begged for mercy. This whole situation was getting out of hand.

"What are you thinking about?" Megan demanded,

as he pulled up at a light. "You look as if you're preparing for battle with that fierce frown. My mother isn't that tough to get along with."

He smoothed out his face at once. "I'm looking forward to meeting your mother. Didn't you say she was in real estate?"

Megan gave him a sharp look, as if she suspected he was deliberately changing the subject. "Yes, and she's very successful at it. She works long hours, but she makes a pretty good living. She had to with three daughters in college and now a son getting ready to go, too."

"What about your father?"

She hesitated, and he felt a pang of sympathy, guessing what she was going to say. "My father died when I was fifteen," she said quietly. "Heart attack. It was all very sudden and a terrible shock."

"I'm sorry," he said gruffly.

"Thank you." She sighed, then added, "My mother worked hard, mostly weekends and nights, to keep the family going. She was gone a lot of the time, and since I was the eldest, I sort of took over for her."

"That must have been tough for a young girl, taking care of four younger kids."

"It was. They were pretty good, but they didn't like being bossed around by their sister. That was Mom's job, and I think they resented me taking over. I had to get really tough with them to get them to listen to me. Things got pretty hectic at times, fighting all four of them. It all worked out in the end, of course. By the time I left high school Mom was making enough to hire a housekeeper."

Tyler was beginning to see where some of Megan's assertiveness stemmed from. She was used to taking charge of a situation without much time to get her point across. He imagined that her mother wasn't the only one good at her job.

"You went to college?" he asked, as they waited at yet another light.

She nodded. "Community college to learn the travel business. I always wanted to travel and that seemed a good way of managing it. What about you?"

"Police academy for basic training, then the department sent me to college for a special law enforcement program."

"Was it hard?"

He shrugged. "Sometimes. I guess the toughest lesson to learn was to separate myself from civilian life."

"Why would you want to do that?"

"It's what every cop has to do. We have to learn to deal with the conflicts between us and the general public."

"Conflicts?" She regarded him curiously. "I don't understand that. Don't people generally respect the police? After all, they expect them to protect them against criminals."

He sent her a wary glance. "The public don't always understand our actions. For instance, they want us to enforce the law, yet if we arrested everyone who broke a law we'd run out of jail space within days. We have to be selective and know what the priorities are. Sometimes there's a thin line between them."

"I can imagine. I never thought about it that way before."

Warming to his subject, he decided to go on. "The public expects us to find and arrest criminals, but doesn't understand that we are forced to follow certain procedures. Those procedures have to be maintained, even if it means letting the suspect escape."

She gave him a guilty look. "Like when that thug snatched my purse."

"Right."

"I see." She was quiet for a while and he wondered if he'd upset her. Then she added in a small voice, "I guess there's a lot that people don't understand about police work."

"What most people don't understand is that we're on a different side of the wall from them. We have to be. We're out there on our own, and we can't rely on the public to help us. A cop is no longer part of the civilian world. He's part of a team, and he has to learn to think like a team. Once you become a cop you lose all civilian identity. It's like you become someone else."

"You must have wanted to be a cop pretty badly."

"I did." He knew she was wondering why he'd chosen his profession. She'd asked him once and he'd evaded the answer. He didn't know if he'd be able to answer her now if she asked.

Luckily he didn't have to make that decision. She pointed out her mother's street just then, and he followed her directions to the apartment building.

"Mom sold the house a couple of years ago," Megan told him as they drew up at the security gate. "She didn't want to have to maintain a house all by herself."

"I can understand that." Tyler wound down the window. "Which button?" He leaned out and pressed the button she'd indicated, and after a moment a pleasant voice said, "Marjorie Summers."

"Tyler Jackson. I'm with Megan."

"Yes, Tyler, come on through."

A buzzer sounded and the gate swung open to allow them to drive through. Tyler watched in the rearview mirror as it closed behind them. "Pretty impressive."

"And pretty expensive," Megan said, making a face. "Too rich for me, I'm afraid. Not that I'd want to live in the same apartment building as my mother and brother, anyway."

She hopped out of the car when he pulled up in the parking space. He followed more slowly, feeling a little apprehensive now that he was about to meet Megan's mother.

He hoped that she didn't get the wrong idea about him. As long as he kept his eyes off Megan, he told himself, Marjorie Summers wasn't likely to notice that her daughter lit up all his lights whenever he so much as looked at her.

All he had to do was keep his attention on the mother instead of the daughter and just maybe he could get through this evening without getting into any deeper water than he was already.

The minute the door opened he knew it was a futile hope. Marjorie Summers was a carbon copy of her daughter. Older, of course, more mature and sophisticated, but there was no denying that when he looked at Megan's mother, he was seeing Megan as she would look at that age. And she was going to be gorgeous.

Chapter Six

Marjorie Summers spent the first few minutes fussing over her daughter's arm, until Megan thought she would go out of her mind. Apart from anything else, it was embarrassing to be treated like a child in front of Tyler. As if she didn't already have enough trouble convincing him she was quite capable of taking care of herself.

Once her mother was convinced that Megan's arm was not about to fall off, she turned her attention to her other guest. "So, Tyler, I understand you are giving my daughter lessons in how to defend herself," she said, after she'd settled him in an armchair with a beer and a plate of cheese snacks.

"I think your daughter is quite capable of doing that already," Tyler said meaningfully. "The first time I met her she knocked me flat on my back."

Megan tried in vain to catch Tyler's eye. She hadn't told her mother about the purse snatching. Too late she realized she should have warned Tyler not to mention it. "Er...how's the real estate market, Mom?" she asked, in a vain effort to change the subject.

"Fine, dear," her mother murmured, her gaze still fixed on Tyler's face. "I'd like to hear more about how you two met each other."

"Megan came to the police station to report her purse being stolen," Tyler said blithely. "She was in a hurry, and so was I. We collided in the doorway."

"Someone stole your purse?" Marjorie Summers said, turning to Megan with her face creased in dismay. "When? Why didn't you tell me?"

"I didn't want to worry you," Megan said, looking pointedly at Tyler.

"That's why she was taking self-defense lessons," Tyler said helpfully, ignoring Megan's fierce frown.

"I just knew something like this would happen." Mrs. Summers turned back to Tyler. "I told Megan when she wanted to get her own place that it wasn't safe for a young woman living on her own in the city. She can be extremely stubborn at times."

"It's perfectly safe, Mom. Besides, I'm not living in the city. I'm living in the suburbs."

"On the wrong side of the river. Why couldn't you find somewhere on the west side to live?"

"I can't afford the west side." Megan sent Tyler a murderous look for getting her into an argument she'd had a hundred times already.

"I think Mrs. Summers is right," Tyler said, reaching for his beer. "It's not safe for a woman to live alone. Especially in that area."

"Oh, please call me Marjorie, dear." She looked at Megan. "You see? Tyler agrees with me."

Megan drew in a deep breath. "Thousands of

women live on their own, Mom, and manage to survive. You will, too, when Gary leaves."

Ignoring that, Marjorie turned back to Tyler, saying chattily, "I keep telling Megan, it's about time she got married. She's not getting any younger, and it's sometimes difficult for a woman to have children once she's past thirty. The trouble is, Megan is so darn independent, she won't admit she needs someone in her life."

Tyler looked as if he wanted to disappear through a hole in his chair.

Mortified, Megan felt her face growing hot. "Mother, I really don't think Tyler is interested in my personal life. In any case, this is all beside the point. My purse was snatched while I was downtown on my lunch break."

"What did I tell you about working in the city?" Marjorie exclaimed. "I don't know why you can't work at one of the travel agencies out here."

"I like working in the city," Megan said, wishing she could reach Tyler's neck to throttle him for starting this whole scenario.

"I suppose you lost your credit cards."

"Yes, but I got them replaced. The worst part was losing all my photos. I'd kill to get them back."

Marjorie shook her head. "What a mess. Were your keys in your purse? I hope you had your locks changed."

She'd forgotten all about the locks, but she wasn't about to admit that. "For heaven's sake, Mother, give me some credit. I'm managing just fine. I've faced far bigger crises than this when I was taking care of my brothers."

Her mother closed her eyes. "I don't think I want to know about that."

"I'm sure you don't," Megan said grimly. "Where is Gary, anyway?"

"In his room doing his homework, I hope." Marjorie looked at the clock. "Dinner's almost ready. Can I get you anything else, Tyler? Would you like to watch TV?"

Relieved that she'd managed to effectively change the subject, Megan headed for her mother's kitchen. "I'll help you get dinner."

"You're not supposed to use that arm, remember?" Tyler called out after her.

"Don't worry, dear. I'll see that she doesn't," Marjorie assured him.

"I'm not about to use it while it's in a sling," Megan muttered under her breath.

"He's very good-looking," her mother said, coming up behind her. "He doesn't look much like a policeman."

"He does in uniform," Megan assured her. "What are we having? It smells great."

"Pot roast. It's all in the oven. I can manage, dear. You really shouldn't be using that arm."

"I can still use the other one," Megan said, opening the fridge door to prove it. "Do you want me to put the salad on the table?"

"If you wouldn't mind. Perhaps Tyler would carve the meat for us?"

"I'll ask him." Megan went back into the living room with the salad bowl tucked in her good arm.

Tyler sat watching a game show on TV. He looked up when she walked in and immediately jumped to his feet. Frowning at her, he held out his hand for the salad bowl. "Let me take that."

"I can manage," Megan said, trying to keep the

edge out of her voice. "Mom wants you to carve the meat."

"Me?" A look of panic crossed his face. "I can't carve meat."

"So wing it." She was beginning to lose patience with both of them. The dining table had been laid with a white cloth, and she dumped the salad bowl on the middle of it, noting her mother's best silver candles placed at each end. Tyler was getting the VIP treatment.

He disappeared into the kitchen, and she heard her mother say something in a low voice which she couldn't quite catch. Tyler answered her, again too softly for her to hear what was said.

Obviously they were talking about her. Megan was about to march back in there to find out what they were saying when her brother bounced into the living room from the hallway.

"Hi, Shortstop. I thought I heard your voice. What'd you do to your arm?"

Megan smiled up at her six-foot-plus brother. "Hi yourself. It's just a pulled muscle, that's all."

"It's not broken?" He sounded almost disappointed. "Where's the cop?"

"In the kitchen."

"Is he armed?"

She gave him a "drop dead" look. "Sorry to disappoint you, but he's not in uniform."

"Bummer." He picked up the remote and pointed it at the TV. Rock music blared into the room, just as Tyler emerged from the kitchen carrying a plate of sliced beef.

"This is Tyler," Megan said, flapping her hand at him. "And would you please turn that racket off?"

Gary shook Tyler's hand and grinned at him. "About time my sister was taken into custody."

"Oh, please." Megan pointed to the head of the table. "Tyler, you sit there. You sit down, too, Gary, and please try to behave like a civilized human being for a while."

Much to Megan's relief, Gary didn't entertain everyone by inventing horror stories about the days when his sister was in charge, as he normally did when he thought it would be fun to embarrass her. Instead, he bombarded Tyler with questions until she felt compelled to protest.

"Let him eat his dinner in peace," she told Gary, after Tyler had related yet another story about his experiences on the street.

Determined to keep her brother's attention off Tyler's hair-raising tales, she asked him how things were going at school.

"Fine," Gary muttered, reaching for another bread roll.

"No, they are not," his mother argued. "His grades are slipping. He spends too much time with his friends and not enough time with his homework."

"I get it done," Gary protested.

"But he doesn't get it done right," Marjorie Summers said, raising her eyebrows at Megan. "I'm tired of worrying about him."

Megan laid down her fork. "You're not being fair to Mom, Gary," she said quietly. "She has enough to worry about without you adding to her troubles."

Gary gave her a rebellious look. "I've got to have some fun sometimes."

"After your homework is done," Megan said firmly. "You're supposed to be the man of the house. If Mom can't rely on you then you're not doing your job. We all took our turn in taking on the responsibility, now it's yours. It isn't as if you have the younger ones to watch out for like the rest of us did. I don't think it's asking too much to at least keep up your grades, do you?"

Gary shrugged one shoulder. "I guess not."

"Great. You'll be glad you did next year when you're picking out a college."

Tyler sat quietly enjoying the excellent meal, secretly amused by the way Megan seemed to take charge of the family. Not content with scolding her brother, she advised her mother on how to deal with a difficult client, and suggested that her sisters join a health club, since they were both having trouble controlling their weight.

She was wonderful to watch, Tyler thought. Mellowed by the good food and a couple of beers, he was beginning to forget his earlier irritation with her assertive disposition.

In fact, he felt a grudging admiration for the way she supervised everyone. Marjorie Summers was right. Her eldest daughter should be married. She was wasting her talents on her family. She should be concentrating all that care and capability on a family of her own.

Not that he was counting himself as the lucky man, of course, he hastily assured himself. He'd learned a long time ago that marriage wasn't for him. But somewhere out there was a man who needed someone like Megan to take care of him.

Tyler wasn't exactly comfortable with picturing the man, however, and he stopped thinking about it and went back to watching Megan's sparring match with her brother.

By the time Megan was ready to leave, Tyler had to admit that he'd enjoyed the evening far more than he'd expected. Far more than was good for him, he suspected, as he thanked Marjorie Summers for her kindness and complimented her on her excellent cooking.

"That was the best meal I've eaten in years," he told Megan, as they headed through the brightly lit streets to her apartment.

She sent him a sideways glance. "I don't suppose you get too many home-cooked meals."

"Not a lot."

"What about Thanksgiving and Christmas?"

He shrugged. "I usually work the holidays, and give the guys with families a chance to take off."

She was quiet for a moment, then said softly, "That's so sad."

She sounded as if she really meant it, and he felt a sudden rush of warmth in his midregion. He tried to brush it off with a casual remark. "You get used to it."

"No. I could never get used to being alone during the holidays."

"You get used to being alone. Period. To some people it's preferable."

"But not to you."

He glanced at her, surprised by the comment. "Why not to me?"

"Because I don't think you really like being alone. Much as you pretend you do. I was watching you tonight. You looked more at ease, more affable than I've ever seen you."

Aware that she was right, he wasn't quite sure how to answer that. "Your mother is an interesting woman to talk to, and I really enjoyed meeting your brother."

"Oh, thanks. That says a lot for what you think about my company."

She'd spoken lightly, but he sensed he'd hurt her feelings. Searching in his mind for some way to make amends, he said hesitantly, "Being with your family like that reminded me of my own brother."

She sat up in her seat. "I didn't know you had a brother. Does he live in Portland?"

Tyler shook his head. He was surprised he'd even mentioned Mason. He'd never talked about him to anyone. "He died," he said quietly. "Several years ago."

"Oh, I'm so sorry. Do you have any other brothers or sisters?"

"Nope. There was just him and me."

She laid her hand on his arm, saying softly, "You must miss him very much."

"I do." More than he'd realized until tonight.

"What was his name?"

"Mason."

"An older brother?"

"Yes." Suddenly he couldn't talk about him anymore. "Thank you for taking me to meet your mother."

If she was surprised at the abrupt change of conversation, she gave no sign of it. "Thank you for driving me there. My mother really enjoyed your company, I could tell."

He felt warm again. In fact, he felt better than he'd felt in a long time. He wasn't sure if it was the beer, the truly excellent meal or the woman at his side making him feel so good inside, and right then he wasn't about to question it. He was just going to enjoy the feeling while it lasted.

Megan was quiet the rest of the way home. So much

so that he began to worry. Usually she chatted nonstop. It wasn't like her to keep silent for so long.

He waited until he had pulled into the parking space in front of her apartment building before saying, "Is something wrong? Is your arm hurting you?"

"What? Oh, no. It's fine."

He could see her face clearly in the reflection cast by the streetlamps. She looked as if she'd been jolted out of some deep thinking.

"I didn't mean it how it sounded," he said awkwardly.

She looked at him in obvious confusion.

"Back there, when I said I enjoyed your mother and brother. I enjoy your company just as much."

Her face cleared. "Oh, that. It's no big deal."

She was smiling at him, her mouth slightly parted to reveal a gleam of white teeth. In the half-light her eyes looked huge and luminous, reminding him for some reason of moonlight on the waters of a tropical bay. Her soft blond hair framed her face, glinting where the lamplight fell across it, turning it to silver.

He was getting poetic again, he warned himself, but for once he didn't want to listen. He wanted to get closer, close enough to smell that intriguing, exotic perfume she always wore.

He shifted closer to her, and saw her face change. It was as if she'd read his mind, before he'd really understood exactly what he was thinking.

Only now he knew what he wanted. What he'd wanted all evening, ever since she'd blushed when her mother had said she should be married. No. Ever since he'd first faced her across the mat in the gym.

He didn't want to think about that right now. He didn't want to think about anything, because if he did, he might chase away the urge that was pressing him closer to her.

She had gone very still, and he could hear her breathing unevenly. He was breathing pretty erratically himself. A tiny part of his mind wondered if he knew what he was getting into. The rest of his mind refused to listen.

He slid his arm across the back of her seat, and heard her catch her breath. He hoped like hell that she wanted what he wanted. Because now he couldn't tear himself away if he wanted to. He was going to kiss Megan Summers here and now, and to heck with the consequences.

Megan felt as if something was squeezing all the air out of her lungs. She had sensed the subtle change in Tyler, and her heart had leaped with anticipation. She wanted him to kiss her, more than she'd wanted anything in a very long time.

She'd been fooling herself up to now, convinced that he thought of her as nothing more than a rather tiresome duty he felt obligated to carry out.

But now he was looking at her as if he saw her for the first time, as a desirable woman instead of an irritating child. That changed things considerably. Now she couldn't wait for him to kiss her. She'd die if he didn't kiss her.

"I guess I'd better see you into your apartment," he murmured, in the husky voice that could make her insides turn cartwheels.

"I guess you'd better." Her own voice sounded weak, as if she'd been running uphill. For once she didn't care.

"I mean, it's getting late and you need your sleep."

He leaned closer, his arm inching across the back of the seat behind her.

"So do you." Her voice was almost a squeak now. If he didn't hurry up and kiss her, she was going to lose it altogether.

"I guess I do." He edged closer, his face only inches away now. "I had a good time tonight, Megan. Thank you."

She started to answer him, but then the world exploded as his mouth gently covered hers.

He wound his arm around her and pulled her closer. Her injured arm prevented her from getting as close as she would like, but she reached up and clasped the back of his neck, just to let him know she was enjoying the kiss.

Then it happened. Softly at first, no more than a faint tinkling. The sound gradually grew louder, until it seemed as if the car rocked with the joyful clamor of them. *Bells. She heard bells!*

The full significance of that hit her with the force of hurricane winds. Stunned by the revelation, she pulled away from Tyler's insistent mouth. "I think I should go in," she said, on a long rush of breath.

He seemed startled, but quickly recovered his composure. "Right. Hang on, and I'll open your door."

"I can open it." She struggled with the handle for a moment, then got the door open and scrambled outside before he had time to reach her. "Don't worry about coming up with me. I can manage."

The all too familiar stubborn look crossed his face. "I'm not going to leave you down here alone. I'm coming up with you. Don't worry, I won't try to put a move on you."

"Of course you won't. I know that." She was afraid

she'd hurt his feelings, but she was in too much of a dither to do much about it right now. All she wanted was to get back into her apartment and have some time to think about the momentous thing that just happened to her.

Tyler was quiet as he followed her up the stairs. He opened the door for her, then handed her the key. "I think I should give this back to you," he said, avoiding looking directly at her.

With a strange little ache inside, she took it. "Thanks. I'll see you tomorrow?"

"I'll be here."

Relieved that he hadn't given up on her altogether, she walked into her living room and sank down on the love seat. She couldn't have heard bells. Yet she had. The loudest, most musical bells she'd ever heard in her life.

The problem now was figuring out what to do about it. She wasn't sure she wanted to be in love with a man who thought he could run her life. She'd had enough of that from her mother. Yet she couldn't deny the way Tyler Jackson had made her feel when he'd kissed her.

She was too tired to sort things out tonight, she decided. She hoped a good night's sleep would help her see things more clearly in the morning.

The only trouble was, she couldn't sleep at all. Every time she drifted off, she dreamed about Tyler and the bells. She'd wake up with a pounding heart and dry mouth, then it would take her an hour or more to go back to sleep, only to repeat the process.

By the time the sun made sleep impossible, she felt as if she'd tramped miles through a wet forest. Her arm ached from all the tossing and turning, and she was dying for a cup of coffee.

She pulled on her robe and drifted into the kitchen. Yawning, she poured water into the coffeepot and set it back on the stand. She added a dash of extra coffee, figuring she needed all the help she could get to wake up. Then she sat down at her dinette table to wait for the coffee to drip.

She was no closer to solving her problem than she was last night, she thought gloomily. Tyler would drive her crazy standing guard over her every minute of the day. Yet when she thought about the men she'd kissed without one single tinkle, she had to admit that what Tyler's kiss did to her last night signified a vital chemistry between them.

Of course, she wasn't sure if Tyler had felt the same thing. He'd seemed to enjoy the kiss, but as usual it was hard to tell how it had affected him. Tyler didn't give much of his feelings away, which was another stumbling block to a successful relationship.

Realizing that the coffee had stopped dripping, Megan got up to pour herself a cup. She could be opening herself up to a lot of trouble by falling in love with Tyler Jackson. If she hadn't already.

Settling back on the chair with the coffee, Megan faced the problem squarely. He'd made her hear bells. No one had ever done that before. She hadn't really believed in the bells until now. She'd simply used it as an excuse not to get involved. Up until now, she'd convinced herself she was better off living on her own.

Now, however, she couldn't deny that what she felt for Tyler was vastly different from anything she'd ever experienced before. She was either in love with the guy, or well on the way. What was it about Tyler Jackson that had captured her heart so unexpectedly?

She thought about that as she slowly sipped her coffee. He was a strong man, full of courage and confidence. She had always admired that in a man. He was caring, concerned about her. Maybe a little too much at times, but he meant well. It was infinitely better than someone who couldn't care less what she did or how she felt.

He was an honest man, and although he didn't say too much about personal things, she had the feeling that when he did, she could trust him to mean it.

That's what it was, she realized suddenly. Trust. He was the first man she'd met whom she felt instinctively that she could trust. Not only with her safety and well-being, but also with her heart. To her, that was everything.

Somehow she knew that he wouldn't have kissed her last night if he hadn't really cared for her. Tyler Jackson wasn't the kind of man to toy with a woman's affections. He'd play it straight down the line. Just one more good reason why she could love him.

Somehow, she had to try to make this work. Now that she'd finally found a man who could ring bells for her, she couldn't let him go without at least giving it a shot.

She put down her coffee cup, frowning in concentration. Maybe, if they had enough time together, she could find a way to prove to him that she was capable of taking care of herself. That he didn't need to worry about her all the time.

She still had several days before she was due back at work. She'd just have to take as much opportunity as she could to show him how independent and self-sufficient she really was.

He had to learn that he didn't have to be responsible for every second of her life. Maybe then, he'd be willing to give her the space she needed. Because unless he did, she couldn't see a happy ending for them.

Tyler, meanwhile, was having his own problem dealing with what had happened. Having slept off the effects of the large meal he'd consumed, he'd woken up to the memory of Megan's warm, pliant mouth eagerly returning his kiss. His body warmed at the thought of it. Until he remembered that she'd broken it off rather abruptly, as if she'd had second thoughts about kissing him.

Well, she needn't worry, he assured himself as he stood under the shower sluicing the cobwebs of sleep away. He'd had second thoughts, too. Big-time second thoughts.

He was beginning to enjoy Megan's company just a little too much. It was easy to get carried away on a warm, summer night in the intimate darkness of a car. Too easy.

It wasn't as if he hadn't enjoyed it. That was the whole problem. He'd enjoyed it too much. Much more of that and he'd be forgetting why he needed to keep her at arm's length.

If he needed a complication in his life, which he didn't, he'd pick a woman who had enough sense to listen to him, which she hadn't. He'd find someone who would understand his concerns, which she wouldn't, and who could accept his advice, which she couldn't. In other words, if he was in the slightest bit interested in a relationship, which he wasn't, it would be with anyone other than Megan Summers.

She was too independent, too darn stubborn to pay attention to him, when he knew perfectly well what he was talking about. He just couldn't live in constant fear of what might happen to the woman he loved. His marriage had failed for that very reason. There was no way on this earth he could go through all that again. No way.

Tyler slapped the soap between his palms so hard it shot out of his grasp and sailed over the shower curtain. Cursing, he stuck a wet foot on the floor outside to retrieve the slippery devil. Already in a foul mood, it didn't help matters when his foot skidded from under him. He struggled to keep his balance by flailing his arms and banged his elbow painfully against the wall.

This, he decided bitterly, was not a good start to the day. It was all Megan's fault, of course. If she hadn't looked at him with that tantalizing smile in the car last night, he wouldn't have given in to the urge to kiss her.

The fact that it wasn't the first time he'd felt that particular urge did nothing to improve his temper. He had sensed that she was trouble that first day when she'd scrambled off his stomach, leaving him feeling as if he'd been zapped by a live wire.

He should have dumped her onto the first officer within reach, instead of falling for that lost and helpless act. There was nothing helpless about Megan Summers. Stubborn and reckless, maybe. But helpless? Not on your life. The problem was, she also thought she was invincible. She refused to listen to reason, and she was going to get hurt, maybe worse. He'd seen it happen too often. He wasn't going to hang around long enough to see it happen to her.

Rubbing his sore elbow, he stepped out of the shower and reached for the towel. He couldn't just walk away from her while she still needed him, of course. But just as soon as her arm was healed and she could do up her bra again... He closed his eyes, shutting out the memory of her smooth, silky back beneath his fingers.

Just as soon as her arm was healed, he amended, he'd be off the hook. His obligation to her would be ended. He could leave with a clear conscience.

As for the kiss, he would simply forget it ever happened. If she had any sense she would forget it, too. If not, he would just have too explain to her, as nicely as he possibly could, that he was just not interested in anything permanent. Knowing Megan, she wouldn't waste time chasing after a lost cause. For if there were ever two people who were totally wrong for each other, it was he and Megan Summers.

Having settled that, he rubbed furiously at his hair with the towel, trying not to think about how she felt in his arms, her exotic fragrance tantalizing his senses and her lips driving him wild.

Chapter Seven

Megan waited with nervous anticipation for Tyler to arrive later that morning. It was Sunday, she told herself, so he was bound to sleep in later.

As the hours passed, however, she began to worry that he wasn't coming back. The kiss last night must have frightened him off, she thought ruefully. Maybe she'd been wrong after all, about the way he felt about her. She might never get the chance to know if things could have worked out between them.

She read the entire Sunday paper, a feat in itself, considering she absorbed very little of it. Staring at a page of advertisements, she wondered what she would do if Tyler had decided to cut short his self-imposed vigil over her.

She'd miss his help with the housework, of course, though she'd pretty much convinced herself that she could manage on her own now. Her arm still ached now and again, but it didn't hurt nearly as much as it had at first.

She'd managed to wrap it herself, fairly securely. She'd even managed to do up her bra, anchoring one end with the injured hand while she fastened it with the other. As for the cooking, considering the problems Tyler had with it, she'd be better off doing it herself.

None of these things really mattered, however, compared to how she would miss him emotionally if he'd decided he didn't want to see her again. It was something she really didn't want to think about.

By the middle of the morning her stomach was complaining so much she decided to eat. She scrambled a couple of eggs and ate them with a toasted English muffin. She had to admit they tasted rather bland after Tyler's imaginative experiments with her spice rack.

She had just rinsed the dishes and stacked them in the dishwasher when he finally arrived, shortly before noon.

"Where's your sling?" he asked her, the minute she'd closed the door behind him.

Relieved at the sight of him, and more happy than she had any right to be, it was on the tip of her tongue to tell him she didn't need it any more. But then that would be defeating her purpose, if she hoped to have him around long enough to work things out with him.

She went back to her bedroom to get it, leaving him in the kitchen to make the coffee. When she came back, he was peering in the fridge.

"What do you want for breakfast?" he asked her, holding up a package of bacon. "I could make French toast again?"

She almost shuddered. She envisioned lumps of soggy bread falling off her fork. Reluctant to tell him she'd already eaten breakfast she said casually, "I'll have cereal and fruit. You go ahead and cook what you want."

She was gratified to see him put the bacon back with a sigh of resignation. "I guess cereal and fruit will do fine."

She grinned at him. "I'm proud of you. I'll get the cereal."

"I'll get the cereal." He pushed her down in a chair. "You stay there."

It was going to be a little tough proving her independence when she wasn't supposed to be using her arm, she thought ruefully, as she watched him fill the cereal bowls. She'd find a way to do it, somehow. In the meantime, she would deal with his overbearing attitude and try not to let it get to her.

He seemed withdrawn while they ate, as if he had something heavy on his mind. She challenged him to a Trivial Pursuit game that afternoon, hoping to recapture the warm coziness they had shared coming home from her mother's place the night before.

Although he seemed to enjoy the game, she could still feel the invisible wall he kept between them. He was just being cautious, she told herself. She had to let him take things at his own pace. He'd relax again, once he knew she wasn't going to pressure him.

There were times over the next three days when she almost lost that conviction. Tyler seemed even more ill-at-ease than usual, and his temper was definitely frayed at the edges. Once or twice he barked commands at her and she had a hard time biting back a scathing comment.

Something seemed to be bothering him, and Megan knew he was deliberately keeping his distance. It was a marked change from the night they'd come back from her mother's, and she couldn't imagine what had caused it.

Apparently he regretted the kiss, since he'd made no effort to kiss her again, much to her disappointment. In fact, he'd hinted more than once that the only reason he was sticking around was to make sure her arm healed properly.

Miserably, Megan had to acknowledge that they were back to square one. Only things were different now. She was in love with Tyler Jackson, and in spite of his distant attitude, she was pretty sure he cared for her, too.

Once or twice she'd caught him watching her with a strange brooding expression. He got nervous every time she got too close to him, and never once asked her how she'd been managing to do up her bra all by herself. It was as if he were holding himself in, afraid to let out what he was really feeling.

She could feel the tension building between them and didn't know what to do about it. It was a relief to have an excuse to go out on Thursday, the day of her appointment at the doctor's office. Tyler was edgy all the way there, barely talking to her as he drove through the heavy traffic.

When he sat down with her in the waiting room he immediately picked up a sports magazine and began idly flipping through the pages.

"You don't have to come in with me this time," Megan told him, when her name was finally called.

To her intense dismay, he merely nodded, his gaze glued to the magazine. "All right. I'll wait out here."

She felt abandoned as she followed the nurse to the cubicle. It wasn't a feeling she was familiar with, and it bothered her a great deal. She had always done things on her own, without a second thought. Why this should be any different she couldn't imagine.

Dr. Hartford's cheery smile greeted her when he swept into the cubicle in a flurry of white coat, stethoscope and clipboard. "Ah, how's the arm? Better I hope?"

"Much better, thanks."

"Still aching?"

"Not any more."

"Still taking the medication?"

She shook her head. "Not for the last three days."

"Good. Sounds as if we are on the mend. Let's take a look."

He undid the sling which Tyler had meticulously tied that morning, and dropped it on the bed. "I don't think we'll need that anymore."

"I'm glad to hear that," Megan said, with a sigh of relief. She watched anxiously as the doctor unwound the bandage, then probed up and down her arm with gentle fingers.

"Hurt here? Here? Here?"

She shook her head.

"Grasp my hand as if you were about to shake it."

She did as he asked, and winced as a spasm of pain zinged up her arm.

"Ah, that hurt."

"A little," she admitted.

"Well, I'm afraid you're going to get the odd spasm or two for some time until the muscle builds itself up again. The only way it's going to do that, of course, is if you use it. Start gradually, and don't put too much pressure on it at first. One small step at a time, that's the secret. If you go too fast you could hurt it again."

"But I can use it again?" Megan asked eagerly.

The doctor smiled. "As long as you're careful with it and it doesn't give you too much pain. If it starts aching again you'll have to rest it for a while. I'd keep it wrapped for another week, just in case. I'll have the nurse give you a fresh bandage. If you have any problem give me a call. Otherwise, you're all set."

Megan thanked him, and he disappeared with a brief wave of his hand. While she waited for the nurse, Megan gave some thought as to what she would tell Tyler.

Once he knew that she could use the arm again, he would no longer have an excuse to stay around. He would go back to being a cop and she would go back to being a travel agent and it was unlikely she would ever see him again, unless she happened to get mugged again.

The ache in her stomach almost doubled her over. She couldn't let that happen. She couldn't just let him walk out of her life without making some kind of effort to give their relationship a chance.

She thought back to that night he kissed her. Things had changed after that. She frowned, going over the whole scene in the car. Of course! She'd pulled away from him when she'd heard the bells. He probably thought she was offended by his kiss and was afraid he'd try something again.

She'd been waiting all this time for him to make the first move, while he was apparently under the impression that she was turned off by him. She had to set things straight right away.

No wait. She couldn't just go barging out there and declare that she was in love with him. What if she'd read him wrong after all? She was taking all this for granted. Not only would she feel like a prize fool if she was wrong, she'd end up embarrassing them both.

It would put Tyler in the very awkward position of having to explain that she was mistaken about his feelings.

Megan huffed out her breath in frustration. What she really needed was more time. If only she had one more week, she could perhaps break through his defenses if she really tried. Show him in subtle ways that she cared for him, without actually hitting him on the head with it. That way, she could find out how he really felt about her.

If she was wrong about him, she'd have to accept it and get on with her life. At least then she wouldn't spend the rest of it wondering if things could have worked out if she'd only given them a chance. On the other hand, if he really did care for her, and was only holding back because he thought she didn't feel the same way, then she had to do something about it.

The door opened and the nurse whisked in, carrying a tray of bandages. "I'm here to wrap your arm," she announced. "The doctor says you should keep it wrapped for another week."

"I know," Megan murmured, her mind still on her problem with Tyler. "He told me." She barely noticed the nurse binding up her arm. As long as she had to keep it wrapped for another week, she told herself, why not let Tyler think she still couldn't use it? That way he'd feel obliged to stick around for a few more days. It would give them a chance to get things straight between them, and could very well change their lives.

A surge of excitement rushed through her at the thought. If she could just get him to kiss her again, this time she wouldn't pull away. This time she'd let him know how much she was enjoying it, and that she wanted him to go on kissing her for the rest of their lives together.

"There you go," the nurse said briskly, as she tucked her scissors into her pocket. "That should hold you for a little while."

Megan thanked her and slipped off the table. She couldn't wait now to get back to Tyler and put her exciting plan into action.

She hurried down the corridor to the waiting room, where Tyler still sprawled on the narrow seat where she'd left him, his nose buried in the magazine.

He looked up as she paused in front of him. "Done already?" His glaze flicked over her arm. "No sling?"

She shook her head. "The doctor said I didn't need it. I still have to keep it wrapped for another week, though."

His gaze barely met hers before glancing away. "Does that mean you still can't use it?"

She hesitated, reluctant to lie to him, then decided it was all for an excellent cause. "I guess so."

He nodded, but didn't say anything as he laid the magazine down and got to his feet. "Then I guess it's back to the cooking lessons."

A stab of guilt hit her and she mumbled, "Well, maybe I could manage that—"

"No way. That's my job until your arm heals." He took hold of her good arm and guided her out to the parking lot and into the car.

He seemed even more tense on the way home, and she kept up an endless stream of chatter in an effort to relax him.

"We need to stop at the store," she said, as they approached the supermarket where she shopped. "I thought we could make tacos for dinner tonight."

"Tacos?" He shot her an anxious look. "Isn't that a bit ambitious?"

She laughed. "No, it's really easy. I'll show you how. I thought we could open up that bottle of wine, too. Now that I don't have to take any more medication. We'll get you some more beer while we're there."

He swung into the parking lot and found a space near the entrance. Controlling the urge to scramble out, she waited for him to open the door for her. She stepped out of the car, and managed to move close enough to him to bump her shoulder into his chest.

"Sorry." She gave him a dazzling smile, practically in his face. "Thank you," she said, lowering her voice to what she hoped was a seductive note.

He looked startled, and slammed the door shut with an almighty thud.

Megan wasn't sure if she'd scored or not. She wasn't used to these kind of tactics. If she used any kind of tactics at all with a man, it was usually in order to get out of a relationship, not encourage one.

This wasn't going to be as easy as she'd imagined, she thought nervously. She would have to be careful she didn't overdo things. She didn't want to embarrass him or herself by throwing herself at his feet if he wasn't interested.

She kept things light while they shopped, and Tyler said very little the rest of the way home. She suggested a board game to pass the time until it was time to eat.

Tyler readily agreed, with such an air of relief that made her wonder if she hadn't been wrong about his reasons for staying aloof.

He seemed even more tense than ever, and twice she had to nudge him to take his turn. He finally ended up winning the game, but even that didn't seem to animate him.

"Are you worried about something?" she asked, as she stood with him in the kitchen while he shredded the lettuce for the tacos.

He gave her a quick glance. "Worried? No, I don't think so. Why?"

She shrugged. "I don't know. You just seem preoccupied lately."

He gave her a half smile. "I guess I'm missing my job. I'm not used to being so inactive."

"I'm sorry, I know having to sit around here all day must be very dull for you."

"Dull?" He shook his head. "I wouldn't say it was dull. After all, I'm learning to cook."

"I'm glad you're getting something out of it."

He looked at her as if he suspected her of being sarcastic. "I'm getting a lot out of it. It's been an...interesting experience."

She wasn't quite sure how to take that. She didn't dwell on it, however, as an idea struck her. "Why don't we do something tomorrow instead of hanging around here."

"Do something?" He paused with his knife in midair. "Like what?"

"Oh, I don't know...the weather is so nice now it's a shame to stay cooped up in this stuffy apartment when we don't have to be." Excitement caught at her as she considered the possibilities. "We could go to the beach, or the zoo—"

"Or a river cruise?"

She stopped short, staring at him in delight. "A cruise? What a fantastic idea! I'd love it."

He went back to slicing thin wedges off the lettuce.

"There's a stern-wheeler that goes through the gorge. The scenery is really something to be seen from the river."

"Oh, Tyler, it sounds wonderful." Throwing caution to the winds, she threw her good arm around his neck and deposited a quick kiss on his cheek. "What a dear you are to suggest it. I can't wait."

He stood perfectly still with his knife poised, staring at the lettuce as if expecting it to attack him. "Is that enough?" he asked, sounding a little strained.

"What?" She peered at the lettuce. "Oh, yes. That's more than enough. Now we have to chop up tomatoes."

"Tomatoes?" He looked at her as if he'd never heard of the name.

"You know, those small, round red vegetables—or are they fruit? I can never remember."

"Tomatoes." He turned to the fridge and opened the door, stared inside for a full five seconds, then took out a couple of tomatoes. "How many?"

"That many," Megan said, feeling somewhat confused. It was obvious she'd caused a reaction in Tyler, but she couldn't be sure if it was positive or negative.

Deciding not to push her luck, she guided him through the rest of the preparations for the dinner, taking care not to touch him again.

Finally the meal was ready, with all the ingredients laid out to fill the taco shells. Megan realized belatedly that since she was keeping up the pretense of not being able to use her arm, she wouldn't be able to fill her own tacos.

Tyler patiently did it for her, then started on his own, while she sat there feeling guilty for making him go through all that when he really didn't need to.

She was almost tempted to admit the truth, but now that she'd already told him a lie, it was a little late to go back on it now without explaining why she did it. Besides, she reminded herself as she bit awkwardly into her taco, she needed this time with him if she was going to get things straightened out between them.

Handling tacos with one hand was proving to be a tricky maneuver, she was beginning to find out. Grated cheese and juicy chunks of tomato fell on her plate, while the spicy meat filling oozed out over her fingers.

Wishing like mad that she could use the other hand, she struggled as best she could to eat the darn things with some modicum of dignity while carrying on a conversation with Tyler about the history of sternwheelers.

It was something of a relief when she finally swallowed the last bite. She dabbed at her mouth with her napkin and gave him a brilliant smile. "They were really good," she said, meaning every word. "You did a great job."

"Thanks."

His rare smile warmed her entire body. She smiled back at him, wondering if she dare lean over and give him another peck on the cheek.

His gaze dropped to her mouth, and she felt her pulse leap in excitement.

"Here," he said quietly. "You missed a spot."

She froze as he reached out and brushed the corner of her mouth. His fingers barely touched her lips, hovering there for a heart-pounding second or two. Then, very slowly, he lowered his hand.

Megan swallowed, then whispered, "Thank you."

"You're welcome."

His voice, low and husky, sent shivers to the very

tips of her toes. His silver-blue eyes seemed to be looking right into her soul, and she wondered if he could see in her face what her heart longed to tell him.

Her breath caught in her throat as she sought the right words. How did she tell a man she loved him when she wasn't sure how he felt about her?

The phone rang suddenly, shattering the magic.

"I'll get it," he muttered, and pushed his chair back from the table.

She watched him pick up the phone, and felt a weird sense of sadness, as if something brief and wonderful had just been extinguished before it really had a chance to begin.

"It's your mother," Tyler said, holding out the phone. "She wants to know how things went at the doctor's today."

Megan got up from her chair and hurried over to him. "I promised to call her when I got home," she said, feeling guilty. "I forgot."

"I'll rinse the dishes while you talk to her."

He disappeared into the kitchen and Megan took a deep breath before greeting her mother.

"Did I hear Tyler say he would do the dishes?" Marjorie Summers demanded.

"Yes, you did," Megan said cheerfully.

"You'd be a very foolish woman to let that one get away," her mother informed her.

Megan heartily agreed, but she wasn't about to say so. Her mother was likely to publish wedding announcements in the paper before the end of the week.

She managed to field her mother's questions about her arm without actually lying, and put the phone down in relief a few minutes later.

When she went into the kitchen, Tyler stood at the

sink, spraying water everywhere as he rinsed the dishes under the faucet.

"My mother says hi," she told him, "and she's madly jealous that you're washing the dishes."

He gave her a little-boy grin that completely melted her heart. "I'll go over and wash hers for another one of her fabulous dinners."

Seizing the opportunity this time, Megan said lightly, "I'll be happy to offer you the same deal just as soon as my arm is better."

He looked at her with interest. "You cook like your mother?"

"I learned from her. At an early age, I might add."

"Oh, right. You cooked for your family."

"You bet I did. My pot roast is every bit as good as my mother's, even if I do say so myself."

"In that case, I might just take you up on your generous offer."

She felt a little rush of hope at his words. Maybe he wasn't planning on walking out of her life, after all.

He went back to rinsing the dishes, and she began stacking them in the dishwasher. "What time will you pick me up tomorrow?" she asked, carefully placing a delicate wine glass on the rack.

"I'll have to check the departure time. We have to drive down to Hood River to pick up the stern-wheeler. I'll look in the paper when I'm finished here."

"I've never been on the river that far down."

He handed her the last plate. "I think you'll enjoy it. It's a nice trip."

"I'm sure I shall. I'm really looking forward to it."

She smiled up at him, and her heart leaped when he said softly, "So am I."

She hid her disappointment later when once again

he left without attempting to kiss her. Maybe she was expecting too much too soon, she told herself, as she got ready for bed.

After all, she still had a week, and anything could happen in that time. Already he seemed to be responding to her efforts. One thing she did know, she wasn't going to let up for one single second. From now on she was going to grab every opportunity that presented itself, and give him all the encouragement he needed. Then it would be up to him whether or not he acted on it.

She just hoped he wouldn't make her wait too long before letting her know how he really felt about her. The suspense was likely to kill her.

Tyler sat in the quiet darkness of his studio apartment, a cold beer in his hand and a momentous struggle going on in his mind.

Something had changed since he left home that morning, and he wasn't at all sure he was comfortable with it. Ever since the night he'd kissed Megan Summers he'd felt as if he were walking a minefield blindfold.

The tension around Megan's apartment had been thick enough to cut, as if the slightest wrong word could light the fuse and set off a blast that would rock the universe.

He found himself weighing every word before he said it, and had done his best to curb his irritation, though he wasn't quite sure what he was irritated at. He'd pretty much convinced himself that Megan was only tolerating him until she could manage on her own again. He'd also managed to convince himself that it was for the best.

Now, all of a sudden, everything had turned around in the opposite direction. If he didn't know better, he'd have said that she was deliberately making a play for him.

It had to be his imagination playing tricks. Which wasn't surprising, since he had his work cut out trying to control his thoughts from straying into forbidden territory.

His biggest mistake was in suggesting the trip upriver. The idea had popped into his mind and the words were out before he'd really thought about it. The cruise was one of his favorite things to do, and his first thought when Megan had suggested doing something together.

It wasn't as if he wouldn't enjoy the trip with Megan. That was the whole point. Every minute he was with her he felt himself sinking deeper into the treacherous warmth of familiarity.

Excitement beckoned to him with every turn of her head, every glance from her gorgeous green eyes. He kept remembering the taste of her mouth under his, and every time she got close to him the urge to kiss her again became almost unbearable.

When she'd kissed him on the cheek earlier, it was all he could do to stop himself from hauling her into his arms. He could feel the pressure ticking away inside him, like a time bomb ready to explode.

He took a swig from the bottle and swallowed it down, trying to get it all in perspective. He was just making a whole heap of trouble for himself. He knew that. When the time came to walk away from her it would be that much harder with every passing day.

Yet he couldn't quit on her now. He had to see it through. And somehow he had to get through this without letting her know how she affected him. Keep things light and uncomplicated, that was the key. Never let down his guard, no matter how much she tempted him.

It was a good thing she wasn't trying to entice him, he thought, as he got up to go to the window. She did enough damage to his composure just by being herself. If she ever did make a play for him, he'd go down like a felled redwood. He'd be putty in her hands. He'd be a dead duck, that's what he'd be. And that would not be good.

He opened the window and leaned out, letting the night wind cool his face. He heard the hum of city traffic, winding its way through the blurry maze of lights—everybody going somewhere from somewhere. The loneliness of his tiny apartment seemed to close in around him. He had never been more aware of the fact that he was on his own.

He withdrew his head, irritated with himself. He was letting himself get maudlin. He'd been on his own for six years now, and he was used to it. He couldn't let one woman mess things up for him again.

For no matter how much she excited him, no matter how much he longed to discover all there was to know about her, he could not get past the conviction that an involvement with Megan Summers was bound to lead to disaster. It just wasn't in the cards. The sooner he accepted that, the better off he'd be.

Chapter Eight

Megan waited impatiently for Tyler to pick her up the next morning. She'd woken up with a tremendous sense of excitement, as if something very special was waiting just around the corner.

She was no longer in any doubt about her feelings for Tyler. She loved him. As she'd never loved anyone in her life. She couldn't imagine life without him now.

She wanted to share everything with him, discover new worlds with him, make a home with him and have his children. Just the thought of having Tyler's children made her feel weak and warm inside.

She couldn't wait to see him again, and watch his smile transform his face over something she'd said. She loved to see him smile, to see those steel-blue eyes light up, banishing the bitter loneliness that she saw too often in his gaze.

All she needed was a little time to show him how good they could be together, and this day promised to offer the opportunity to do that.

She stood at the window, her heart skipping a beat every time she saw a car pull into the parking lot. By the time she finally saw Tyler's car nose into a parking space, her nerves were wound as tight as a canning lid.

She watched him climb out, one long leg appearing first, then his dark head before he unwound the rest of himself. He closed the door and scanned the parking lot all the way around before heading over to the building in his easy stride.

Ever the cop, Megan thought, smiling. Always checking out the territory. He'd been taught to be observant in every aspect of his life. How could he not know that she was head over heels in love with him?

Well, he'd know by tonight, she promised herself. Or at the very least, he'd have a good idea how she felt about him.

The doorbell rang and she flew to the door, anticipating his smile when he saw her. Having listened to the forecast for a very warm day, she'd dressed in khaki shorts and a sea-green sleeveless shirt.

Now that she could use two arms, she'd managed to get her hair back in its usual smooth style, instead of the flyaway arrangement that had sufficed for the past week. It had been sheer luxury to use some eyeshadow again, and she was happy with the result, confident she was looking a lot more presentable than she had the past few days.

She opened the door eagerly, smiling from the pure pleasure of looking at Tyler's face again.

He wore jeans and a dark blue polo shirt, and looked wary, as if he wasn't quite sure what to expect from her. His glance slid over her in quick appraisal. "Hi, you ready?"

"I've been ready for ages." She followed him down

to the car, and waited for him to open the door for her before climbing in.

"I thought we'd stop for pancakes on the way," he said, as he pulled out into the street.

"Sounds good to me." She settled back in her seat, prepared to enjoy the day.

The restaurant he chose was one of her favorites, and she ordered the blintzes. She watched Tyler consume bacon, eggs, a stack of pancakes loaded with syrup, and felt compelled to warn him about his cholesterol count.

"When was the last time you had it checked?" she asked, as they resumed their journey down the gorge toward Hood River.

"My last checkup, a year ago."

"And was it high?"

"No higher than it usually is, I guess."

She shook her head at him. "You really should watch what you eat."

"I'll bear it in mind."

She felt a pang of uneasiness and sent him a sideways glance. He was back to being distant again. Was it something she'd said? She searched her mind, but couldn't think of anything that might have upset him.

Deciding it was her imagination, she leaned back to enjoy the scenery. Towering walls of craggy rock soared toward the sky on either side of the wide Columbia River. Every now and then crystal-clear water gushed and cascaded down, splashing between the spindly pines that clung to their precarious hold on the slippery slopes.

A light haze hung over the gorge, turning the distant rocks a grayish-blue. Above them, a hot, blue sky promised a cloudless day. Perfect weather to be on the river.

"Did you bring suntan lotion?" Tyler asked, as they swept along the fast highway alongside the river.

"I did." She opened her purse and took out the tube of cream to show him. "I need some help to put it on my left arm, though."

She could have easily managed it herself, but she could hardly tell him that. Besides, the thought of Tyler's fingers rubbing suntan lotion on her arm was too pleasurable to miss.

"I'll take care of it when we get there."

He'd sounded gruff and she frowned. This was not going the way she'd planned. She'd just have to try harder.

They arrived in the little town of Hood River in plenty of time to board the stern-wheeler. Tyler led her to the front of the boat, where they would have a clear view of the magnificent scenery surrounding them on all sides.

"You'd better put this on me now," Megan said, handing him the suntan lotion. "I'll burn easily out on the water."

He took the tube from her and squeezed some into his palm. "I see you're managing to wrap your arm yourself," he said, as he smoothed his palm down her bare skin.

Megan caught her breath as a delicious tingle pervaded her body. "Yes," she said unsteadily. "It took a few practice runs, but I'm getting pretty good at it now."

"So I see." He concentrated his gaze on his fingers as he moved them in small circular motions down her arm.

She bit her lip in an effort to prevent a moan of pleasure from escaping.

"You're also getting pretty good at dressing yourself," he said quietly.

She gave him a sharp look, but he was still concentrating on her arm. "It's taking me a lot longer of course, but it's amazing how you can manage to find ways to do things when you have to."

He nodded. "Amazing."

Her uneasiness grew. What was he getting at?

She was about to ask him outright when he asked casually, "You're not using your injured arm to do things, by any chance, are you?"

Guilt swamped her, and she knew her face was getting red. She never was any good at lying. She was beginning to hate this pretense. Fortunately she was saved from answering by the deafening blast from the stern-wheeler's whistle.

"I guess we're off," Tyler said, handing her the suntan lotion.

"Great!" She dropped the tube into her purse and leaned against the rail, watching in fascination as the huge craft headed slowly out to midstream.

Tyler knew a lot about the river and its history, and spent the next hour or so pointing out interesting landmarks and fascinating facts that kept her enthralled. He showed her the nest of a bald eagle and shortly after she was thrilled to see the bird itself perched in the branches of a lofty pine.

"You must have studied this area quite a lot to know so much about it," she remarked, after he'd explained how the pioneers had floated everything downriver on rafts in order to reach the end of the Oregon Trail.

"The history of this place fascinates me," he said,

leaning his elbows on the rail beside her. "I can imagine how all this must have looked to the pioneers, after traveling for six months across the country to get here. After some of the places they'd been through, Oregon must have seemed like paradise."

"Once they'd crossed the mountains, anyway."

She leaned her back against the rail and looked at him. His dark hair was ruffled by the wind, and the sun had deepened his tan. The banded sleeves of his shirt clung to his muscled arms, and the open neck bared his throat.

He looked so much more relaxed now, almost boyish in his pleasure of the magnificent surroundings. She felt a great rush of tenderness, so much that her throat closed up.

He chose that moment to glance up at her. Some of her feelings must have shown in her face, as his expression changed. He gave her a slow smile.

She smiled back. "Pretty impressive, isn't it?"

"Very." His gaze wandered down to her mouth, making her feel suddenly breathless.

She looked away from him, to where the eagle now soared above the trees, gliding just above the branches. "It's all so quiet and peaceful, it's hard to believe we are so close to the city. You can almost sense how the pioneers must have felt, seeing it all for the first time."

"There's so much land out there." He straightened up, his hand resting lightly on the rail next to hers. "It's hard to imagine how those people literally walked over two thousand miles of it."

Megan looked down at his strong, tanned hand lying so close to hers. Obeying the impulse that was impossible to ignore, she laid her hand on top of his. "Thank you for bringing me here today, Tyler. This is the best time I've had in ages."

He stared down at their linked hands for a long moment, then to her utter delight, he gave her a wide grin. "Me, too. I guess I owed you this for everything you've been through this last week."

She shrugged. "I told you my getting hurt wasn't your fault. It was as much mine for not paying attention. I feel kind of bad though that you gave up your vacation to take care of me."

"There's no need to feel bad. I had nothing better to do, anyway. It was good to get away from the job for a while, and besides, I got free cooking lessons."

"And you were probably bored out of your skull."

Her pulse leaped when he lifted her hand, studied it for a moment, then raised it to his mouth and lightly kissed her fingers. The hungry warmth in his eyes made her heart beat faster. "No," he said, in his husky voice, "I wouldn't say I was bored at all."

"Well, I enjoyed having you around," she said cautiously. "I'll miss you when it's over."

A brief cloud passed over his face, but his voice was light when he said, "I don't want to think about going back to work. Let's just enjoy the day and to heck with tomorrow."

"That sounds like a great idea." She'd matched his tone, though inside a little niggle of doubt worried her. She didn't want to examine her thoughts too closely, for fear of what she might find there. All she knew was that in those brief words, she'd heard a note of finality. She didn't want to think about what that might mean.

"I used to take Mason down to the river in Bend when we were kids," Tyler said, turning back to the rail.

The last time he'd talked about his brother, Megan had sensed that it was a painful subject for him. Thrilled that he felt like talking about it to her, she said carefully, "I bet you both had fun."

Tyler nodded. "We did. We used to imagine we were on a pirate ship sailing out to sea. We'd spend hours fighting off rivals, or making invisible mutineers walk the plank. We'd go home with our clothes wet and muddy, and my mother would yell at us and send us both to our rooms, but we couldn't wait to come back and do it all over again."

Megan laughed. "It was worth getting into trouble for, right?"

"Every bit of it." His smile held more than a hint of sadness. "I think Mason really believed that one day he'd sail away on a pirate ship and never have to come back to the real world."

Her heart ached for him. "Perhaps he did."

He looked taken aback, and stared at her, as if she'd said something profound. After a moment he said in a strange voice, "I like that. It makes it easier somehow."

She was terribly afraid she was going to cry. She wanted to put her arms around him, to hold him close and never let him go. She wanted to tell him everything she felt in her heart, and somehow find the words to tell him how much she loved him.

All she could do was say quietly, "I'm glad. I know what it is to lose someone."

He nodded. "Your father. That must have been tough."

"It was. It was so sudden. I adored him, of course. I remember looking at him the day of the funeral. I just couldn't believe that he wasn't playing an elaborate joke on us, and wouldn't suddenly jump up and laugh at us all for being so easily taken in."

"I know what you mean. It's impossible to believe that someone you love could be taken from you like that, and there's not a thing you can do about it."

She nodded, tears stinging her eyes.

He reached out and caught one with the tip of his finger. "Sorry," he said gruffly, "I didn't mean to get you depressed. This trip was supposed to give you a break and take your mind off your troubles."

She managed a smile. "To give us both a break. And it's wonderful. I'm so glad you suggested it."

He wiped the last of her tears from her cheek with his thumb. For a moment his fingers rested against her neck, and she brushed her chin over them in a soft caress.

His eyes seemed to catch fire as he gazed at her. "Me, too," he said softly.

Somehow, deep inside, she knew she would remember that moment for the rest of her life.

The day passed quickly after that. When the sternwheeler arrived back at the landing stage, Tyler suggested stopping off at Multnomah Falls on the way back.

They climbed halfway up the falls in the dry heat of the afternoon before giving up the struggle, and raced each other down again, teasing and laughing for most of the way.

Tyler was ahead by the time they reached the last stretch and he waited for her at the bottom, arms outstretched as she laughingly stumbled toward him.

Without giving herself time to think she ran headlong into him, and he caught her close against his heaving chest. Too far out of breath to speak, she rested her cheek against his shoulder until her lungs stopped gasping for air.

He held her close, panting heavily himself, until she pulled her head back to look up at him. "That's what I get for not working out lately," she said breathlessly.

"Me, too." His voice sounded strained, and now her heart was pounding for a very different reason.

She stood quite still in the circle of his arms. His mouth hovered just above hers. His face was serious as he stared down at her, and the warmth once more burned in his eyes. Seconds passed while she silently willed him with all her strength to lower his mouth to hers. Then his expression changed abruptly, and he let her go.

"Let's take a look in the gift shop," he said, pulling her by her hand toward the small store at the side of the lodge.

Shaken by the depth of her feelings, she went without protest. She felt dazed, as if she'd just woken from a deep sleep, as she followed him around the store. Her emotions had been on a roller coaster all day, swooping up and down with such velocity she felt weak and dizzy.

One minute she was filled with glorious hope, the next dashed to the ground with doubts. If this was what being in love felt like, she wasn't too sure she wanted to deal with it.

Not that she had much choice, she thought, as she paused to look at the souvenir books on a stand at the back of the store. It was too late to back out now. She'd waited all this time for the right man to come along, and now that he was here, she was hooked. There was no going back. She was in love with Tyler Jackson, and she would be in love with him for as long as she lived.

On impulse, she bought a book filled with pictures of the gorge for Tyler. When she caught up with him he handed her a lapel pin, a miniature replica of the stern-wheeler.

"Just a reminder of a great day," he said, smiling at her as she exclaimed with delight.

"It's lovely. Pin it on my collar for me, please?"

He did so, standing there in the middle of the store, with people milling around them, his fingers warm against her skin as he fastened the pin.

His face was close enough to kiss, but she curbed the impulse. Instead she breathed in the faint fragrance of his aftershave, and filled her mind with the memory that would be hers to keep, no matter what happened between them.

Tyler once more lapsed into long periods of silence as he drove up the freeway toward the city. They stopped for hamburgers on the way, and although he answered her comments, he seemed preoccupied.

He appeared to be wrestling with some deep thoughts, and Megan couldn't help wondering if he was trying to come to terms with their relationship.

Her stomach felt as if it were full of rocks by the time they reached her apartment building. She could only hope and pray that he would make the right decision, because she really didn't know what she would do if he chose to walk away from her now.

She waited in an agony of suspense for him to say something after he'd parked the car and cut the engine.

For a while he said nothing at all, then he sat back in his seat and let out his breath on a long, slow sigh. "I have a couple of errands I have to run in the morning, so I probably won't be here until around lunchtime. Do you think you can manage until then?"

Again she was overwhelmed with guilt. "Of course," she said quickly. "Please don't worry about me."

If only he would look at her, she thought anxiously. If she could look into his eyes, maybe then she could tell what he was thinking.

He sat so long in silence she felt she could stand it no longer. "Well," she said, doing her best to sound indifferent, "I'd better go in. Thank you for a wonderful day, Tyler. I really had a good time."

He looked at her then, and the torment on his face made her feel like crying. "So did I."

She nodded, her throat aching with the effort not to break down. "Well, good night, then."

He reached for her so suddenly she was taken completely by surprise. His kiss was hard on her mouth, insistent, demanding and just a little desperate. But oh, so sweet.

She gave herself up to it, winding her good arm around his neck and kissing him with all the pent-up feelings she'd been holding onto all day. It was so wonderful to let go of them, and she put her heart into it.

When he finally drew back, she was as breathless as she'd been on her way down from the falls.

"I'll take you to the door," he said thickly, and climbed out of the car.

Still trembling, she waited for him to open the door and help her out. The night air felt chilly on her bare arms after the heat of the day and she shivered.

"Cold?" He curled his arm around her and held her close to his side as they slowly climbed the stairs together to the second floor.

She clung to the moment, enjoying the warm, secure feeling of his body so close to hers. He paused at her door, and she fished the key out of her purse and handed it to him.

He opened the door for her and gave the key back to her. "Good night, Megan." He bent his head and gently touched her lips in a kiss that was all too brief.

She couldn't bear the thought of this incredible day ending. For some reason she felt that once she let it go, the new and fragile closeness they had shared that day would disappear with it.

"Want to come in for a beer?"

She hadn't really expected him to take her up on the offer, and she wasn't really surprised when he shook his head.

"It's late, and I should be getting back."

"Okay. I guess I'll see you tomorrow then."

He gave her one of his deep, brooding looks, then brushed her cheek with his fingers. "See you," he said quietly, and then turned and headed for the stairs.

He didn't look back as he turned the corner, and she felt a deep sense of loss that she couldn't explain as she let herself into the apartment.

She had never felt so alone when she walked into her empty living room. She couldn't shake the melancholy, although she didn't understand why she should feel so depressed.

Tyler had kissed her, not once, but twice. She'd achieved what she'd set out to do. She just wished he'd seemed as happy about it as she felt. She had the impression that he was still holding back for some reason. If only she knew what it was.

She'd had her own doubts at first, but at least she was reasonably sure she could make things work between them. There had been times that day when it seemed as if Tyler agreed with her. But then something always seemed to get in the way, bringing the doubts rushing back again.

It didn't help that she felt guilty for keeping up the pretense of being unable to use her arm, she thought, as she got ready for bed. If there was to be real trust between them, there should be no lies, no matter how well intentioned they were.

Lying in her bed, staring at the darkened ceiling, she decided she would have to tell him. Tomorrow, just as soon as he arrived at the apartment. She would tell him that her arm felt so much better that she had started using it again. Then it would be his decision whether or not he went on seeing her, now that she no longer needed him to care for her.

She couldn't bring herself to tell him that the doctor had told her to use her arm yesterday. That would mean explaining why she'd chosen not to tell him that. She didn't want to put him in the awkward position of having to explain why he couldn't love her. It would be better for both of them if he never knew how she really felt about him.

Megan groaned and rolled over onto her side. No one had told her that being in love could be so complicated. She'd always imagined that one day she'd meet the man of her dreams, they'd fall in love and get married, have children and live happily ever after.

Never once in that scenario did she ever imagine that the man of her dreams wouldn't love her back. That possibility just hadn't occurred to her.

She dashed a tear away with an impatient hand. She was being melodramatic and immature. She didn't know that Tyler couldn't love her, she was just assuming things. Just because he hadn't dropped to his knees and begged her to marry him didn't mean he didn't care for her.

Men like Tyler were cautious. He'd been hurt by the failure of his first marriage and wasn't going to rush into anything this time. She couldn't blame him for that. Her problem was that she was too impatient. She wanted everything now. Whereas Tyler needed time.

She sighed into the quiet darkness of her bedroom. She'd be willing to give him all the time in the world as long as she knew there was hope. If only he'd say something that she could hang on to. Then again, the look in his eyes when he'd kissed her had been everything she could have wanted.

She just had to be patient, she told herself, and not expect too much too soon. Once Tyler knew she could fend for herself again, she'd finally know where they stood. And if it turned out that she'd been wrong about his feelings for her, then she'd have to deal with it and get on with her life without him.

She woke up suddenly, surprised to find the night had flown and sunlight was once more warming the room. As always, things seemed so much better in daylight.

She would tell Tyler about her arm, she decided, and then she would invite him to stay for dinner. She would cook him a pot roast, since he'd seemed to enjoy it so much at her mother's house. After the simple meals they'd shared lately, he'd probably appreciate it.

She scribbled down a list of things she'd need. She'd have plenty of time to go to the store, she decided, and be back before Tyler arrived. She could have most of the meal prepared by then. She might even have time to bake a lemon meringue pie before he got there, as a special surprise.

Excited about her plan, she drove to the supermarket and shopped for what she needed. It seemed strange to be out on her own again. She missed being with Tyler. She missed his dry comments and sarcastic humor. She missed the sheer excitement of anticipating what he was thinking, and the thrill of trying to read what might be behind his teasing remarks.

She paid for the groceries, and followed the clerk out to the car, where he loaded the heavy sacks into the car for her. Except for the occasional spasm, her arm had held up just fine. She should be able to carry the groceries in without any problem, she thought, as she pulled into her parking space.

The warm summer wind tugged at her hair when she walked around to the trunk and opened it. There were more clouds in the sky today, and the sun had lost the fierce heat of yesterday. The summer would soon be over, Megan thought, as she lifted a sack out of the car. Then it would be back to the rain.

Deep in thought about the coming fall, she failed to see Tyler until he stepped in front of her.

She jerked to a stop, rattling the jars in the sack she carried. "Oh, Tyler! I didn't see you. You're early. I wasn't expecting you until noon."

"So I noticed." He scowled at the sack in her arms. "I see your arm's all better."

"Yes, I—"

"Just when were you figuring on telling me?"

She felt her face growing warm. "I was going to tell you when you got here. It felt so much better I started using it again. So I decided to cook you a special dinner tonight and I needed things from the store...."

Her voice trailed off as he brushed past her and hauled out the other two sacks. "And you couldn't wait for me to get here," he said bitterly, as he strode past her with the sacks in his arms.

She followed him up the stairs, her heart thumping against her ribs. She should have waited, she thought belatedly. She'd been so excited about surprising him she hadn't thought about how he'd feel. It must seem as if she couldn't wait to get rid of him so that she could be out on her own again.

She was still trying to think of the right words to say when she reached the door. It stood ajar, and Tyler had disappeared inside. She could hear him in the kitchen as she crossed the living room.

He was unloading the sacks onto the kitchen counter when she walked in. "I'm sorry, Tyler," she said, as she set her sack on the counter. "I just didn't think. I was hoping to surprise you."

"You surprised me all right." He slapped a package of frozen vegetables on the counter. "I've spent the last nine days waiting on you hand and foot so you wouldn't have to use that arm, and the minute my back is turned you're out there doing your best to mess it up again."

She felt terrible. She couldn't tell him the truth about her arm without admitting why she'd lied to him, which certainly wouldn't help matters any, judging by the look of fury on his face. "My arm does feel a lot better," she said cautiously, "and I was careful with it."

"Careful?" He waved an angry hand in the air. "You call that careful to drive all the way to the grocery store with an injured arm? What if you'd had to swerve to avoid something? How good do you think you'd do with one hand?"

"Tyler, it's only a few blocks."

"I don't care if it's only a few feet. It was taking a chance you didn't need to take. What about your arm? How do you know what damage you might have done by carrying a weight like that before the muscle is properly healed? How do you think I'd feel if you messed it up for good? I'd have that on my conscience. You might at least have warned me you were planning on doing something that reckless."

"Reckless!" Stung by his tone, she glared at him. "For heaven's sake, Tyler, it wasn't that far. You're worrying over nothing."

He nodded, his mouth drawn tight with resentment. "Nothing. Well, I've heard that before."

"I'm sure you have. You seem to have a habit of anticipating trouble. You have to start trusting people to think for themselves now and again. I'm perfectly capable of judging my limitations."

"Is that right? Is that why you sneaked out behind my back? To test your limitations without me there to stop you?"

Incensed enough to retaliate, Megan thrust her chin in the air. "If you weren't so darn overprotective, hovering over me all the time like an anxious new mother, I wouldn't have to sneak out behind your back."

His eyes turned to steel as he glared at her. "Well, if that's how you feel, that can be easily remedied. From now on, sweetheart, you're on your own. Don't come crying to me if your arm gives out on you and you can't use it any more."

"You'd be the last person I'd go to."

"Fine."

"Fine, then."

He stared at her for a moment longer, then cursed under his breath and marched across the kitchen to the door.

Her anger evaporated as fast as it had arisen. "Where are you going?" she demanded, beginning to panic now that he was leaving.

He paused in the doorway, hesitated, then turned around to face her. His anger seemed to have vanished as well, leaving a weary, resigned look on his face that frightened her far more than his fury. "I'm going back to work," he said quietly. "I have a feeling I've been away from it far too long. You know where to find me if you need me."

She nodded, feeling a sick ache inside that she knew was not going to go away. "I'm sorry, Tyler."

"Yeah," he said bitterly. "So am I."

She waited until she heard the door close, before sinking down at the dinette table and burying her head in her arms for a good cry.

Chapter Nine

Megan spent the next two days moping around the apartment, telling herself what a lucky escape she'd had. Who needed an overgrown nursemaid, anyway? She'd always managed perfectly well on her own, and she could go on taking care of herself.

She certainly didn't need a man around to tell her how to live her life, she told herself. She even managed to convince herself she meant it.

She started a new jigsaw puzzle and scrapped it before she'd even got all the outside pieces in place. She called her mother twice, and hung up before she had a chance to answer. She cooked the pot roast and barely touched it, finally deciding to wrap it and put it in the freezer.

By the end of the second day she was tired of hoping the phone would ring, jumping out of her skin when it did, then crashing with disappointment when it wasn't Tyler.

She was tired of staring at the phone, fighting the

urge to call him and ask him to come over. Not that it would do any good anyway. He'd never see her as a responsible adult, capable of making smart decisions and sensible choices. He'd always treat her as a reckless, ignorant child, which was an insult to her intelligence. She simply couldn't live with that.

The best thing she could do, she told her reflection that night, was to go on with her life and forget she'd ever met Tyler Jackson. They would both be better off.

Getting back to work was a great relief to Tyler. It helped keep his mind off his problems. He didn't want to think about Megan's smile, or her warm, green eyes sparkling at him in the reflection of sun-kissed waters.

He didn't want to remember her lithe body slithering over his shoulder onto the mat, or hurtling into his arms at the side of the rushing falls.

He didn't want to envision the wind in her hair as she stood at the rail of the stern-wheeler, and he didn't want to feel the memory of her lips eagerly returning his kiss. Most of all, he didn't want to listen to poetic terms repeating over and over in his mind.

He didn't want to, but he kept doing it anyway. No matter how hard he stared at the reports, no matter how much he concentrated at the wheel of the squad car, no matter how determined he was to fall right to sleep at night, the memory of her laughter, and the soft touch of her hand kept intruding into his thoughts until he thought he would go out of his mind.

Halfway through the second night, when he found it impossible to go back to sleep, he went to the bathroom and confronted his image in the mirror.

He had to get a hold of himself. He had to write the whole thing off to experience. She wasn't going to listen to anything he said, no matter how right he was. She had a mind of her own, just like Katy. He would have the same problems he had before, and he couldn't handle them then.

The best thing he could do for both of them was to go on with his life and forget he'd ever met Megan Summers. They would both be better off.

Megan woke up the next morning full of good intentions. She called the travel office and told them she would be back to work the next day. Her suits were ready to pick up at the cleaners, her library books were due back, and her hair badly needed a trim. She could take care of everything that day, she decided, and go back to work with a clean page in her calendar.

She climbed into her car, relieved to have something more constructive to do than sitting around waiting for a phone call that would never happen. The sooner she got on with her life the better, she told herself as she drove to the library.

She was due to go to Japan next month, and she had that to look forward to. With the kind of job she had, it wouldn't do to get too involved with anyone, anyway. As long as she was on her own, she was free to take advantage of the opportunities that came up.

It would be good to get back to work, she thought, as she pulled up in front of the library. She enjoyed her job, and she missed everyone at the agency.

Beginning to feel just a shade better, she climbed out of the car and reached in for her books. As she straightened again, she glanced across the street and nearly dropped them. A man hovered in the doorway of the appliance repair shop. A man who looked frighteningly familiar.

Megan narrowed her eyes, just to make sure. About five-eight or nine, skinny, with long, dark, straggly hair. He was still dressed in the jeans and dark jacket he'd worn two weeks ago. There was no doubt in her mind. She was staring straight at the man who had stolen her purse.

Her first instinct was to rush right over there and demand that he give back her purse. Fortunately she had enough sense to realize the futility of that.

The next thought that occurred to her was that he was probably waiting for another unlucky victim to come by with a purse swinging from her shoulder. In which case, she should attempt to warn someone.

The police, of course. She should call the police.

Now that she had a legitimate excuse to call Tyler, she was strangely reluctant to do it. She didn't want him to think she was running after him or anything.

Torn with indecision, she watched the man in the doorway for another moment or two. He kept sticking out his head to look down the street.

She had to get out of his sight, she told herself, tossing her books back in the car. He could easily recognize her, and take off, and she'd lose him again. Besides, she couldn't just ignore him and let him snatch someone else's purse.

Having made up her mind, she pushed her way through the doors of the library and headed for the phone.

She half hoped that Tyler wouldn't be there when she called. That way the decision would be made for her. When she asked for him, however, after a moment's pause, his deep, husky voice came on the line.

"Jackson here. What can I do for you?"

Her knees weakened at the sound, but she resolutely

lifted her chin. "This is Megan. I'm at the library and I've just seen my mugger."

There was the barest of pauses, then Tyler asked crisply, "Where is he?"

"He's across the street, in a doorway." Her voice had a slight tremble in it, despite her best efforts to keep it steady. "I think he's waiting to mug someone else."

"You're sure it's him?"

"I'm positive. I told you I'd know him right away if I saw him again."

"Right." Another small pause. "I'm coming out there."

Her pulse leaped. "All right."

"I want you to stay in the library, Megan. Do not go out there. Do not attempt to speak to him. Just stay out of sight. Is that clear?"

Now he sounded like a cop, she thought wryly. "I understand."

"Do what I say, Megan. Please."

That had sounded a little more personal and her heartbeat quickened. "I will, Tyler, just hurry, please. I don't want him to get away this time."

"I'm on my way."

The line went dead and she hung up the phone with a shaking hand. What if the man had a gun? What if Tyler got shot? It would be her fault. How could she live with that, knowing she was responsible, no matter how indirectly?

Her stomach churning, she peered through the glass door at the appliance store. He was still there. She almost hoped he would leave before Tyler got there, then scolded herself for being a coward.

Tyler wouldn't want him to leave. That was his job,

apprehending criminals. No matter how dangerous. He was used to dealing with scum like that.

She swallowed, her gaze fixed intently on the purse snatcher. She wished now she hadn't called Tyler. She should have just ignored the man and forgot she saw him. But then that would be shirking her duty as a responsible citizen. She couldn't ignore what was right just because Tyler might get hurt.

She straightened up with a little gasp. The man had stepped out into the street, and was looking up and down as if expecting someone.

Megan's mouth went dry. What if he'd seen her call and had guessed she'd called the police? Maybe he was even now waiting for Tyler, ready to shoot him on sight. No, wait, he'd stepped back into the doorway.

Megan barely had a moment to catch her breath when the man stepped out again and began walking rapidly away from the store. With a little cry of dismay, she bounded out of the library.

A quick glance down the street told her that Tyler still hadn't arrived. The mugger was leaving. He was going to get clean away.

Megan ground her teeth. This animal was marching off, free as a bird to snatch someone else's purse and put them through the misery she'd had. The loss of her money, the hassle to get new credit cards, new driver's license, new social security card and new keys had taken up all her spare time for days. Apart from anything else, the loss of her precious photos had really upset her. They were irreplaceable.

Megan shot one last hopeful look down the street. Still no Tyler. She looked in the other direction. The mugger was already two blocks away. If she didn't do something, she'd lose him. Without giving herself time to change her mind, she set off at a quick pace after him.

When Tyler arrived at the library a few minutes later, Megan had disappeared from view. He wasted several minutes searching the library for her. The librarian finally told him that she'd seen a woman answering Megan's description, but that she'd left.

At her words, Tyler knew a fear that he'd never felt before, in all the years he'd been on the force. She must have gone out to confront the mugger. She could be in his hands right now.

They could have gone in any direction. He had no way of knowing. If she was in trouble he was helpless to save her. She was on her own.

Sickened by the thought of what might have happened to her, he rushed out to his car and flung himself into it. He'd cruise the streets all night if he had to, but he had to find her. Somehow, somewhere. All he could pray for was that he found her alive and unhurt.

Megan kept close to the storefronts as she followed the mugger's brisk pace. Every now and again he paused to look into a display window, and when he did she darted into a doorway, holding her breath until she dare peek out to see if he was moving again.

Twice she almost lost him when he crossed the street, and once he disappeared around a corner. Afraid to go charging around it in case he was waiting for her, she waited a little too long. By the time she edged carefully around the corner he was at least three blocks away.

She had to run like mad to catch up with him, and

barely caught sight of him as he turned yet another corner, heading uphill toward the park.

Obviously purse snatching wasn't too profitable, Megan thought irritably, if the man couldn't afford a car. Unless he'd parked it off the street somewhere. If that was so, all she had to do was get the license plate number and Tyler would have his man.

She wasn't going to get any closer to him, she promised herself as she slowed to a walk again. She wasn't really sure what she was going to do. If he didn't have a car she could tail him until he got home, so that she'd know where he lived. Then she could inform Tyler, he could arrest the mugger, and maybe get her purse back. Or at least the photos. Then Tyler would have to admit that she was capable of handling situations on her own. She really liked that bit.

She hoped that the man would reach home soon. She was beginning to get tired, and a little niggling pain in her side was bothering her. With all the sitting around she'd done lately, she was really out of shape. First thing tomorrow, she promised herself, she'd get back to her aerobics routine with her videotape.

She was so busy thinking about everything that she almost missed the mugger's next move. She was walking across the street from the park when she noticed he'd gone. For a moment it seemed as if he'd simply vanished in the wind, but then she caught sight of him in the park walking briskly up a path through the trees.

She had to wait for the light before she could cross the street. Once more she had to force herself into a fast trot to reach the path, by which time the mugger had completely disappeared.

She couldn't have lost him, Megan thought in frustration. He had to be around somewhere. He couldn't have gone far in the short time it had taken her to get across the street.

The path curved up the hill and disappeared into a thick stand of trees. He had to be somewhere up there. For a moment she hesitated, remembering what Tyler had said about going after criminals.

But all she was doing was following the man. He didn't even know she was behind him. She was pretty sure he was heading for the parking lot at the top of the hill, which was where he'd probably left his car, hidden away from the eyes of the city police.

She wouldn't have to get that close to him. A description of the car and the license plate number should be more than enough for Tyler to pick up the trail. Now that she was this close, she hated to give up. Especially if she could get her photos back. More especially if she could win Tyler's respect.

Taking a deep breath, she ran up the path.

A few blocks away, Tyler radioed his report to Control, and asked them to notify him of any calls coming in. His stomach felt tied up in knots. It was a familiar feeling. He'd felt the same way when he'd worried about his ex-wife.

Only now the ache was more like an agony, gnawing away at his insides like a rat trapped in a wall. If anything happened to Megan... He shook his head. He couldn't let himself think that way. He needed all his concentration.

His heart seemed to leap into his throat when he caught sight of a slender woman with light blond hair crossing the street in front of him. Almost immediately, his spirits plummeted again when he realized it wasn't Megan.

Damn her, he thought, pounding the wheel with his fist. Why couldn't she do what he'd told her? Why couldn't she just have stayed put, instead of charging off all on her own? What in the hell did she hope to accomplish? All she was going to do was get herself hurt. Maybe badly.

If he could only find her, he thought, as he anxiously scanned the people on either side of the streets, he'd sit her down and give her a lecture she wouldn't forget. If only he could find her.

All at once he found himself praying. That was something Tyler Jackson didn't do very often.

Back in the park, Megan trudged breathlessly up the hill, anxiously scanning the trees ahead for any sign of the mugger. He'd had a good start, she thought, as she approached a sharp curve. He could already be at the parking lot. If so, he could be gone before she could catch so much as a glimpse of his car.

She tried to speed up, gasping as the pain bit deep into her side. In an attempt to ignore it, she concentrated on her surroundings.

Sunlight dappled the leaves of the dogwoods and sliced between the trunks of towering firs on either side of her. A slight breeze stirred the branches, hardly enough to cool her burning face. The pungent smell of damp wood and mossy earth added to the sense of being deep in a forest, and being alone.

She switched her thoughts to the parking lot, which she knew lay a few more yards up the hill. Almost there. She rounded the curve, and every nerve in her body froze in shock. The mugger stood directly in front of her, blocking her path.

The man stared at her, his dark eyes cold and cruel. Megan mentally backpedaled, although fear held her to the spot. Frantically she searched her mind for something to say, anything that would get her out of what was turning out to be a dangerous situation.

She forced her lips back in a grisly smile. "Er, do you happen to have the time?"

The man narrowed his eyes. "You were following me," he said, in a rasping voice that sent unpleasant shivers down her neck. "All the way from downtown."

She sent a desperate glance around in the vain hope that someone was close enough to hear her. If she screamed, would anyone hear her? If people heard her would anyone investigate? Even if someone did, it was doubtful he'd get there in time to stop this thug from hurting her.

"What do you want?" the man demanded. "Why are you following me? Are you the law?"

A brief vision of Tyler popped into her mind. He had warned her. She hadn't listened. "No, no," she said, vehemently shaking her head. "I just wanted to know the time, that's all. I'm sorry I bothered you."

"Not nearly as sorry as I'm going to make you," the mugger growled, taking a step toward her.

Megan backed away again. "Now, look," she said, doing her best to sound imperious, "there's no need to get nasty."

He gave her a horrible grin, baring a mouthful of crooked yellow teeth. "No need to get nasty," he mimicked her in a high-pitched voice. Then his expression changed to a fierce scowl and his voice dropped to a raspy growl again. "Lady, you ain't seen nasty until you see what I can do."

She swallowed, and slowly slid her purse from her shoulder. "Here, if this is what you want, take it."

A flash of recognition crossed his face, turning her

blood cold. "I seen you before," he said, moving his hand to the inside pocket of his jacket. "I remember you now. So that's your game, huh? Figuring on turning me in, is that it? Well, lady, you just made the biggest mistake of your life."

Megan's stomach gave a sickening lurch when she saw the knife in his hand. She was too tired to run. He could easily outpace her with his long legs, in any case. There was only one thing left to do. She just prayed she could remember how to do it right.

She dropped her purse and backed away from him, bracing herself with her feet planted firmly apart. Remembering Tyler's sharp commands, she forced her muscles to relax, even though her heart pounded so badly it seemed to vibrate right through her head.

The sunlight glinted on the knife as the man raised his arm. Megan kept her gaze fixed on it, and made a sudden move to the left, as if she were going to make a run for it.

The mugger lunged, and she let out a fierce blood-curdling yell with all the force her lungs would allow. Taken by surprise, her attacker briefly broke his stride.

Megan made a frantic grab for his upraised arm, and twisted her body away from him. Hauling on his arm, she doubled over. Her shoulder jabbed him in his armpit.

He didn't exactly sail over her back the way he was supposed to. It was more like a clumsy, stumbling trip.

She was supposed to complete the move by holding onto his arm and wrenching it up behind him so that he couldn't get away, then stick her foot in his neck to keep him down.

It had looked so easy when Tyler did it.

It wasn't easy at all, she discovered. For one thing,

the man's weight landed squarely in the middle of her back, sending her sprawling. She thrust out her arms to save herself and hit the ground with a jolt that rattled her teeth. A red-hot spasm of pain shot up her right arm. At the same moment she heard the sickening crack of a skull meeting something solid.

Scrambling to sit up, she saw the mugger on the ground a few feet away. He lay on his back, his head resting on a fallen limb, his eyes closed.

For a frightening moment or two she thought she'd killed him. No matter what he might have intended to do to her, she didn't think she could live with his death on her conscience for the rest of her life. But then, she noticed his chest slowly rise and fall.

The relief was overwhelming. Shaken by the ordeal she bent low over her injured arm, cradling it to her.

She had to get out of there, she thought dimly, before the mugger woke up and attacked her again. There was no way she could defend herself now.

She couldn't seem to find the strength to move, however, and she stayed there on the ground, rocking back and forth in an effort to ease the pain.

Vaguely she heard a siren in the distance, but didn't really connect it until it drew closer, becoming almost deafening before it shut off amid a loud squeal of brakes. The noise had come from the top of the hill above her, and she peered up through the trees, trying to see beyond them to what must be the parking lot.

Her heart missed a beat as a tall, dark-haired cop appeared at the top of the hill. Completely disregarding the path, he plunged down the steep slope toward her, sliding to a stop just a few feet from her.

She thought at first she was imagining things. But it

really was Tyler bending over her, his voice harsh with anxiety. "Where'd he get you?"

She couldn't see his eyes behind the sunglasses, but she could see the terror in his face. "I'm all right, Tyler," she said quickly. "It's just my arm. It went out on me again."

His face crumpled for just a second, as if he were about to cry, then the grim mask was back as he turned to the man lying a few feet away. "What happened?"

"He came at me with a knife." Her voice trembled and she cleared her throat. "I tried to remember what you taught me and tried to throw him. I didn't do it properly but he hit his head when he fell."

"Lucky for you," Tyler said grimly. He reached for his belt and unhooked the handcuffs. "How'd he get you here?"

Megan fidgeted nervously. "I sort of followed him from the library."

He turned on her, hot anger blazing in his eyes. "You followed him into the park? Are you nuts?"

"I saw him leave the doorway and I thought—"

"I know what you thought." He leaned over the unconscious man and snapped the cuffs around both wrists. "You thought you'd take care of this all by yourself."

She flinched at the coldness in his tone. "It wasn't like that, Tyler. I saw him leave and I was afraid he'd get away again. All I meant to do was follow him to his car or something...."

Her voice trailed miserably off into silence as she watched Tyler examine the man on the ground. The mugger stirred and groaned, just as another siren wailed in the distance.

"Is he all right?" Megan asked anxiously.

"He'll live."

"He must have hit his head pretty hard when he fell." She shuddered at the memory.

"You were lucky," Tyler said grimly. "If he'd bounced back you wouldn't have stood a chance."

"I know." She peered up at him, wishing she could see his eyes. "I'm sorry."

A shout interrupted them just then, and another police officer appeared through the trees. Tyler waved to him, and he came slithering down the hill toward them.

"How bad is the arm?" Tyler asked, hooking his hand under Megan's left elbow. "Can you get up?"

"Sure." With his help she scrambled to her feet. "I just needed to rest for a moment." She did her best to hide her grimace of pain, but Tyler's quick look of concern told her he'd noticed.

The cop reached them, shaking his head at the mugger, who was struggling to sit up. "What happened?"

Tyler briefly explained. "I need you to take Megan up to my car while I read him his rights," he said, giving her a stern look. "You wait for me there," he ordered, "and stay there until I get there."

She felt like saluting. Instead she gave him a brief nod and followed the officer up the path to Tyler's car, which was parked at an odd angle across a parking space.

A small group of people stared at her as the friendly officer put her into the car. "They probably think I'm being arrested," she said, nodding at the curious onlookers who were whispering together.

"More likely everyone's talking about how you overpowered the suspect. One of the guys over there called in on his cell phone. He and his wife saw the whole thing from up here."

"I didn't know anyone was up here or I'd have yelled my head off," Megan said, beginning to feel self-conscious.

"Well, you must have yelled anyway, because that's what they heard. You attracted their attention just in time for them to see you send the guy flying. You impressed the heck out of them."

Megan shook her head. "It was more luck than anything else. I feel like a fraud."

He grinned at her. "Don't worry, they'll forget about you as soon as they see Jackson bring up the prisoner. You might as well enjoy your brief moment of glory."

She felt more like crying, she thought, as she settled herself in the back seat. Her arm ached, her side ached, and Tyler was furious with her. She just wanted to go home and forget this whole thing ever happened.

It seemed ages before Tyler finally appeared, pushing the stumbling man ahead of him. She heard an outbreak of applause from the group, and someone cheered.

Tyler ignored them, his expression carved in granite.

Megan couldn't hear what he said to the other officer, but he must have asked him to take his prisoner to the station, as the cop pushed the mugger into the back of his car and slammed the door.

Megan watched Tyler stride toward her, his face still a grim mask. She felt like jumping out of the car and making her own way home, if only she'd had the strength.

He climbed in the front seat and started the engine without so much as a glance at her.

Now that there was nothing else to see, the crowd was beginning to wander away. Megan felt immeasurably depressed. She might have disobeyed Tyler's orders, but she had single-handedly disarmed a dangerous criminal. He could at least give her credit for that.

He said absolutely nothing as he drove out of the park and onto the freeway. Megan could tell by the way he sat stiff-backed in his seat that he was still upset with her. She kept quiet until she realized that they had passed the off-ramp to her apartment.

"Where are we going?" she demanded, beginning to resent his silence.

"To the hospital to have that arm checked out again."

She sighed. "There's no need for that. It will be just fine after I've had a chance to rest it."

"I'll let the doctor decide that, if that's all right with you."

She winced at the sarcasm in his voice. "If you insist."

"I do insist." He was quiet for a moment, then burst out, "What the hell did you think you were doing? After everything I said, I can't believe you deliberately risked your life for a stupid purse."

"It wasn't the purse," Megan muttered. "It was the photos. I didn't want anyone else to go through what I did and lose something that meant that much to them."

"If it isn't him it's going to be someone else. There are dozens more like him out there on the streets. You can't win the war on crime all by yourself by putting away one man. You sure as hell can't win by getting yourself killed."

"I wasn't planning to try anything dangerous," Megan protested hotly. "How was I to know he would realize I was following him? I was so careful."

"Men like that can spot a tail a mile off. Following him into the park just clinched it. Didn't it even occur to you that he could be waiting behind a tree for you? You were damn lucky he jumped you from the front. He could have come directly at you from behind and you'd never have known what hit you."

She didn't answer, and he swore as he braked hard to avoid a pickup that cut in front of him. "Damn it, Megan, you could have been killed out there."

He was right, Megan thought miserably. She'd been so busy trying to gain his respect she'd ignored the risks. She could be dead by now, lying under a tree in the park with her throat slit. Her mother would never have forgiven her. As for Tyler, it was unlikely he'd ever forgive her either. It looked as if she'd really blown it this time.

Chapter Ten

An unfamiliar doctor with thick red hair and a strong Scottish brogue greeted her a few minutes later. He raised his eyebrows at her when she explained everything that had happened.

"Well," he said heartily, "it sounds as if you've had an interesting afternoon."

He didn't know the half of it, Megan thought miserably. She'd just spent the worst few hours of her life, and had blown her one chance of happiness. Things couldn't be much worse.

She watched anxiously as the doctor examined her arm. All she needed now, she thought, was for him to tell her she'd be permanently disabled. That would make the whole day just perfect.

To her relief, he straightened up with a smile. "You were lucky, young lady. No permanent damage, as far as I can see. You've aggravated the injury, but it should be all right as long as you rest it. I don't think you need a sling, but try not to use it for a day or two. I'll have the nurse wrap it, just to make it more comfortable."

Megan sighed. "It was just beginning to feel better."

"Well, you'll just have to curb your swashbuckling for a while." The doctor looked at her with a piercing blue gaze that reminded her of Tyler. "If I were you, lassie, I'd leave that sort of thing to the police from now on."

"Don't worry," Megan assured him as she slid off the bed, "I intend to. That was just a little too close for comfort."

She walked slowly back to the waiting room where she'd left a grim-faced Tyler. She could understand how he'd felt. She'd felt much the same way when she'd worried about the mugger shooting him.

All she'd wanted to do was prove to him that she could handle her life very well without him having to hover over her every second. Now she'd only made matters worse. He'd never respect her now. She'd well and truly blown it.

"What's the verdict?" he asked her, when she walked up to where he stood at the window.

"It will be fine after a day or two. I just have to rest it, that's all."

"Is that the doctor's opinion or just yours?"

She flushed. "The doctor's. So you don't have to worry about it anymore."

"Where's your car?"

"It's still at the library."

"I'll take you home and have someone pick up your car."

"Thanks, I appreciate that."

She followed him out to the car, her heart aching in misery. He sounded so abrupt, so fed up with her. She couldn't really blame him. She had to find some way to make him understand how sorry she was for causing him so much trouble.

She waited until they were once more out on the freeway before saying the words she'd rehearsed in her mind. She glanced at him, but couldn't tell much from his expression. He seemed so far away, his gaze concentrated firmly on the road.

"Tyler," she said hesitantly, "I'm sorry for being such a pain. I guess you were right, I did something pretty stupid. I know I should have waited for you to get there. I know I shouldn't have gone after the mugger on my own."

Apart from a slight tightening of his mouth, he gave no sign of having heard her.

She pulled in a breath and tried again. "I just want you to know that I've learned my lesson. I'll never do anything like that again, I promise. From now on I'll be more careful. You don't have to worry about me anymore."

Still no response. Refusing to give up, she went on doggedly, "I know I've caused you a lot of trouble, and I won't bother you again, but I would like to finish the lessons on self-defense. I realized when I tried to throw that brute that I still have a lot to learn, and I'd really feel more secure if I knew what I was doing."

She saw his eyebrow twitch and went on hurriedly, "I'm not planning on using it against anyone, or anything like that. It's just as a precaution, in case I should ever need to defend myself."

Much to her dismay, he still didn't answer her.

"I understand, of course, if you don't want to give them to me." She looked hopefully at him, willing him to look at her. "What I'm asking you to do is sign me up for the fall classes. My arm should be fully healed by then."

When there was still no response, she sank back in her seat, feeling as if her whole world were crumbling around her. There was no doubt about it now, she'd really blown it. The only man who'd ever made her hear bells and she'd lost him.

She sat in silence until they reached the parking lot of her apartment building. Tyler nosed the car into the parking space and braked, bringing them to a standstill. She braced herself to say goodbye to him, determined not to let him know how much she was hurting inside.

She turned to him, ready to say the words that would allow him to walk out of her life. To her surprise, he shut off the engine and opened his door.

"You don't have to come up with me," she said quickly, terrified she'd break down if he didn't leave right now. "I'll be all right."

"I'm coming up with you."

She watched him slam the door and stride around the hood. He didn't touch her as she climbed out, and she led the way up the stairs to her apartment, praying that she'd hold on to her composure long enough to say goodbye.

"I do want to thank you for everything you've done," she said as they reached the top of the stairs. "I really don't know how I would have managed last week without your help."

He paused in front of her door and held out his hand. "Give me your key."

She swallowed, trying to get rid of the hard lump that had formed in her throat. If he didn't leave now, she thought frantically, she was going to make a complete ass of herself right in front of him. Her voice sounded strangled when she spoke. "Tyler, I can manage."

He held out his hand. "The key, please."

She chewed her lip. He was still treating her like a child. That would at least make it a little easier to say goodbye. A little, but not a whole lot.

She dug in her purse with her left hand and found the key. She handed it to him and he took it without a word. She waited in silence for him to open the door, then walked past him into her living room.

Filling her lungs with air, she turned to face him. "Thank you, Tyler," she said stiffly, "for everything. I really appreciate everything you've done for me." She held out her hand for the key.

Instead of giving it to her, he stepped inside the room and closed the door, standing with his back pressed against it.

Not another lecture, she thought, staring wearily into his set face. She couldn't stand one more word. She'd done everything she could do, now it was over. She'd had about as much as she could take.

"If you're going to remind me of all the terrible things that could happen to me on the streets of Portland," she said bitterly, "forget it. I've had enough lectures, and heaven knows enough hands-on experience to last me a lifetime. I know you don't trust me to tie my shoelaces, but then that's not really your problem, is it?"

He opened his mouth to say something, but she was on a roll and she wasn't about to give up now. "From now on I'm just another citizen, another one of those members of the public who rely on the police and expect them to perform miracles when in reality they are just as human as the rest of us. That's not your fault, so from now on, you can forget I ever existed and go back to your work with the satisfaction of knowing you have made the world safer for one enlightened woman.''

"Will you please shut up?"

She snapped her mouth shut and stared at him. The purposeful gleam in his eyes made her heart start to race. She wasn't sure what that look in his eyes meant, but she desperately wanted to know. "Tyler, I—"

Her words ended on a gasp as he stepped forward and pulled her hard against his chest. "Did anyone ever tell you," he said softly, "that you talk too much?"

Before she could recover enough to answer him, he effectively prevented her from saying anything at all by covering her mouth with his.

Surprise, relief, delight and excitement followed in quick succession as the bells clamored joyfully and unbelievably loud inside her head.

Although he was obviously being watchful of her injured arm, he somehow managed to hold her tightly enough to squeeze all the breath out of her lungs. Not that she minded, of course. She was happy to expend her last breath on him just as long as he would go on kissing her with such satisfying passion.

She felt decidedly light-headed when he let her go, as if she were floating three feet above the carpet. If this was love, she thought, gazing up at his wonderful face, she wanted to wallow in it forever.

"Now that we've got that straight," Tyler said, in an amazingly matter-of-fact voice, "I've got a few things I want to say."

He led her to the love seat, and pushed her gently down on it. She went eagerly, anxious to know what it was he wanted to tell her. He sat down next to her, put his arm around her and drew her into his side.

He was quiet for a moment, his expression serious. She watched his face, suddenly afraid that her joy had been premature. Then he started to speak in a hushed voice that unsettled her.

"When I got to the library this morning," he said, "and you weren't there, I nearly went out of my mind. I can't tell you the ugly pictures my imagination conjured up. All of them highly possible. I was frantic."

"I'm sorry," she started to say, but he touched her lips with his fingers.

"No, let me finish. Being a cop has certain disadvantages at times like these. I've seen so many terrible things, it's easy to imagine the worst. Especially when I got the report that a woman had been attacked in the park. Somehow I knew it was you."

She felt bad. She remembered how she'd felt worrying about Tyler getting shot.

"The report said that the mugger was down," Tyler went on, "but that the woman was injured. I couldn't get any more than that. I kept imagining you lying on the ground with a bullet in you, maybe dying. I couldn't get there fast enough."

He leaned his head back and closed his eyes. "In those few minutes it took me to get to the park, I realized just how much you meant to me. I was facing the possibility that I could lose you, and I knew then just how miserable my life would be without you."

He opened his eyes again and looked down at her with a rueful smile. "I spent a lot of time trying to kid myself, Megan, but I can't fight it anymore. I love you."

Tears filled her eyes. She loved him so much. It was

overwhelming to know that he felt the same way. "I love you, too," she whispered.

"I was hoping you did." He dropped a gentle kiss on her mouth, barely brushing her lips. "I never would have forgiven myself if anything had happened to you."

"It wouldn't have been your fault, Tyler."

"I would probably have found a way to convince myself it was my fault."

She sat up, moving out of his arms. This was important, and if they were ever going to find happiness together, it had to be settled between them here and now. "You just can't go around making yourself responsible for everyone you meet," she said, laying her hand on his arm. "Everyone has to take responsibility for themselves. Even children have to learn that they are responsible for their actions."

"Some of them can't be," Tyler said. He massaged his forehead with his thumb and forefinger. "My brother, for instance. He was born with Down's syndrome. He relied on me for just about everything."

She uttered a cry of dismay. "Oh, Tyler, I'm so sorry."

He shrugged. "Just one of those things. Mason was three years older than me, but it seemed more like the other way around. I kind of watched out for him. He had a rough time with the kids in the neighborhood, and needed someone to stand up for him."

"So you protected him," Megan said, beginning to understand.

"I guess. I would have died for him if I had to, and I know he felt the same way about me. When he died…"

His voice faded, and Megan reached for his hand and clung to it.

"When he died," Tyler repeated after a long pause, "he was only nineteen. I was devastated. I couldn't understand why the sweetest, gentlest, most affectionate person I'd ever known had to die so young. I felt as if I'd let him down somehow. That there must have been something I could have done to save him. He depended on me, and yet I'd let him down in the worst possible way."

Tears spilled down Megan's cheeks as she pictured the sixteen-year-old Tyler's grief. "You didn't let him down, Tyler, how could you?"

He nodded. "I know. His heart just gave out. But it didn't stop me from torturing myself with guilt. Even now, I find myself wishing I could explain to him that I was powerless to help him."

"I'm sure he knows." It sounded trite, she knew. She wanted so desperately to find the right words of comfort. They just weren't there.

"I hope so. I guess when he died it made me realize how vulnerable we all are. Life is pretty fragile when you think about it. It can be all over in a second. Nothing teaches you that better than being a cop, unless it's a stint in the military."

"You can't dwell on it, Tyler. It must make your job very difficult."

He shrugged. "You get fatalistic about it, I guess. If the bullet's got your number on it, there's nothing you can do about it, so why worry."

She smiled. "So you worry about everyone else instead, is that it?"

"I guess I do."

"And that's why you became a cop. To protect people."

"Something like that."

She lifted his hand to her mouth and pressed her lips to it. "I'm sorry about Mason. It must be terrible to lose a brother so young."

"We were lucky to have him as long as we did. He was a really wonderful person, always so eager to please and so ready to give everything he had to those he loved."

"He wasn't afraid to love."

He gave her a rueful glance. "No, he wasn't."

She lowered his hand again. "I'm so sorry I worried you so much, Tyler. I guess I really wanted to show you how well I could take care of my life without you around to constantly protect me."

He sighed. "I guess I did go overboard on that. Bad habit of mine."

"Well, you were right in this case. I could have done with some of that protection in the park. I thought I knew what I was doing, but I didn't. If that mugger hadn't hit his head when he fell, I'd have been in real trouble."

"I'm glad you realize that. I don't want to sound like a broken record, but don't ever tackle anyone unless it's your last resort. In most situations, unless you think your life is in danger, it's better to submit than fight."

Megan pulled a face. "I don't submit easily. Besides, he came at me with a knife."

He clamped his arms around her and held her tight. "I know. But most petty crooks stay away from murder, unless they're strung out on drugs. He was probably just trying to frighten you."

"Well, he certainly succeeded," Megan said with feeling. "From now on I'll leave the police work to the people who know what they're doing, instead of trying to play Superwoman."

Tyler chuckled. "All things considered, you handled it pretty well."

"I was lucky."

"I'm not going to argue with that." He pulled her toward him and kissed her soundly on the mouth.

"I hope this doesn't mean that you won't trust me out on my own again?" Megan said lightly.

Tyler's smile faded. "As a matter of fact, I did some pretty deep thinking about that while I was waiting for you in the hospital."

She eyed him warily. "And?"

He leaned back, and folded her hand in his. "Once I'd finally admitted to myself how I really felt about you, I knew that if I was going to make you happy, I would have to accept the fact that I can't be responsible for you every minute of the day. I know you need your own space to make your own decisions, and I have to respect that. I have to trust you to know what's best for you."

Feeling a rush of tenderness, she leaned over and kissed him. "Thank you."

"It's not going to be easy," he warned, shaking his finger at her. "Don't test me too much at first. I'm likely to forget now and again."

She shook her head. "I won't test you at all, Tyler. I understand now why you feel so protective and I'll try to respect that, too. If we both work at it, we'll be okay."

"I know we all have to make mistakes in order to learn," Tyler said soberly. "Like with the cooking."

Megan raised her eyebrows. "The cooking?"

"Yeah, I learned from my mistakes. That's how I learned to cook."

She didn't have the heart to tell him he still had a long way to go before he could challenge Julia Child.

"I know everyone needs their own space if they are to grow," he said, pulling her close to hug her. "I'll learn to live with that, but I can't promise to stop worrying about you."

"I hope you won't have to." She kissed the tip of his nose. "I'll pay more attention to you from now on."

He grinned at her. "What the heck did I do to get so lucky?"

She smiled serenely back. "You made me hear bells."

"I did?" He narrowed his eyes. "You know something, I think I heard them, too, when I kissed you at the door. Maybe I should kiss you again, just to make sure?"

"I think that's a wonderful idea," Megan said happily.

His kiss made her forget about everything except how wonderful it was to be in his arms. After a long time he lifted his head, and Megan regarded him anxiously.

"Well?"

He slowly nodded his head. "Bells."

"Really?"

"Definitely bells. You know something else?"

She snuggled up close to him with a happy sigh. "What?"

"They sounded a lot like wedding bells."

She was suddenly afraid to breathe. "Does that frighten you?"

"Only if you refuse to marry me."

With a squeal of delight she flung her arms around his neck. "Oh, Tyler. You are going to make my mother so happy."

"Hey, I'm not planning on marrying your—"

She smothered the rest of his words with a very long, satisfying kiss. There was no longer any need for either of them to say more. Things wouldn't always be easy for them, she knew that. But as long as she heard bells when he kissed her, she'd face whatever life with Officer Tyler Jackson might bring.

Something told her their future was going to be quite wonderful.

* * * * *

Don't miss Doreen Roberts's next book,
THE MAVERICK'S BRIDE,
an exciting new story
in her RODEO MEN series,
coming to Silhouette Intimate Moments
in August, 1999!

Silhouette ROMANCE™

SOMETIMES THE SMALLEST PACKAGES CAN LEAD TO THE BIGGEST SURPRISES!

Join *Silhouette Romance* as more couples experience the joy only babies can bring!

Bundles of Joy

July 1999
BABIES, RATTLES AND CRIBS... OH MY!
by Leanna Wilson (SR #1378)

His baby girl had suddenly appeared on his doorstep, and Luke Crandall needed daddy lessons—fast! So lovely Sydney Reede agreed to help the befuddled bachelor. But when baby cuddles turned into grown-up kisses, Sydney wondered if what Luke really wanted was *her!*

August 1999
THE BILLIONAIRE AND THE BASSINET
by Suzanne McMinn (SR #1384)

When billionaire Garrett Blakemore set out to find the truth about a possible heir to his family's fortune, he didn't expect to meet a pretty single mom and her adorable baby! But the more time he spent with Lanie Blakemore and her bundle of joy, the more he found himself wanting the role of dad....

And look for more **Bundles of Joy** titles in late 1999:

THE BABY BOND by Lilian Darcy (SR #1390)
in September 1999

BABY, YOU'RE MINE by Lindsay Longford (SR #1396)
in October 1999

Available at your favorite retail outlet.

Silhouette®

Look us up on-line at: http://www.romance.net

SRBOJJ-D

Looking For More Romance?
Visit Romance.net

Look us up on-line at: http://www.romance.net

Check in daily for these and other exciting features:

Hot off the press
View all current titles, and purchase them on-line.

What do the stars have in store for you?

Horoscope

Hot deals
Exclusive offers available only at Romance.net

Plus, don't miss our interactive quizzes, contests and bonus gifts.

PWEB

THE FORTUNES OF TEXAS

This BRAND-NEW program includes 12 incredible stories about a wealthy Texas family rocked by scandal and embedded in mystery.

It is based on the tremendously successful *Fortune's Children* continuity.

Membership in this family has its privileges...and its price.

But what a fortune can't buy, a true-bred Texas love is sure to bring!

This exciting program will start in September 1999!

Available at your favorite retail outlet.

Silhouette®

Look us up on-line at: http://www.romance.net

PSFOTGEN

Silhouette ROMANCE™
twins on the doorstep

STELLA BAGWELL

continues her wonderful stories of the Murdocks in Romance & *Special Edition!*

MILLIONAIRE ON HER DOORSTEP—May 1999
(SR#1368)

Then be sure to follow this miniseries when it leaps into Silhouette Special Edition® with Sheriff Ethan Hamilton, the son of Rose and Harlan. Discover what happens when a small New Mexico town finds out that...

PENNY PARKER'S PREGNANT!—July 1999
(SE#1258)

Judge Penny Parker longed to be a mother, but the lonely judge needed more than the sheriff's offer of a "trial" marriage....

Look for a new Murdocks short story in Silhouette's Mother's Day collection, coming out in
May 2000

Available at your favorite retail outlet.

Silhouette®

Look us up on-line at: http://www.romance.net

SRTWINS

Coming in July 1999

Back by popular demand, the very first Man of the Month title, plus two brand-new short stories!

DO YOU TAKE THIS MAN?

by
bestselling authors

DIANA PALMER

ANNETTE BROADRICK

ELIZABETH BEVARLY

He is friend, lover, provider and protector. He's as sexy as sin. And he's all yours!

Celebrate the 10th Anniversary of Silhouette Desire®'s **Man of the Month** with the story that started it all and two brand-new stories featuring sexy, superb heroes, written by three fabulous authors.

Available at your favorite retail outlet.

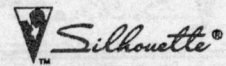

Silhouette®

Look us up on-line at: http://www.romance.net

PSDYTTM

THE MACGREGORS OF OLD...

#1 *New York Times* bestselling author

NORA ROBERTS

has won readers' hearts with her enormously popular MacGregor family saga. Now read about the MacGregors' proud and passionate Scottish forebears in this romantic, tempestuous tale set against the bloody background of the historic battle of Culloden.

Coming in July 1999

REBELLION

One look at the ravishing red-haired beauty and Brigham Langston was captivated. But though Serena MacGregor had the face of an angel, she was a wildcat who spurned his advances with a rapier-sharp tongue. To hot-tempered Serena, Brigham was just another Englishman to be despised. But in the arms of the dashing and dangerous English lord, the proud Scottish beauty felt her hatred melting with the heat of their passion.

Available at your favorite retail outlet.

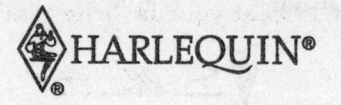

HARLEQUIN®

Look us up on-line at: http://www.romance.net

This August 1999, the legend continues in Jacobsville

DIANA PALMER

LOVE WITH A LONG, TALL TEXAN

A trio of brand-new short stories featuring three irresistible Long, Tall Texans

GUY FENTON, LUKE CRAIG and CHRISTOPHER DEVERELL...

This August 1999, Silhouette brings readers an extra-special collection for Diana Palmer's legions of fans. Diana spins three unforgettable stories of love—Texas-style! Featuring the men you can't get enough of from the wonderful town of Jacobsville, this collection is a treasure for all fans!

They grow 'em tall in the saddle in Jacobsville—and they're the best-looking, sweetest-talking men to be found in the entire Lone Star state. They are proud, hardworking men of steel and it will take the perfect woman to melt their hearts!

Don't miss this collection of original Long, Tall Texans stories...available in August 1999 at your favorite retail outlet.

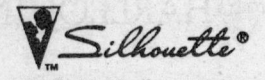

Silhouette®

Look us up on-line at: http://www.romance.net

PSLTTT